Amy Cross is the author of more than 100 horror, paranormal, fantasy and thriller novels.

OTHER TITLES
BY AMY CROSS INCLUDE

American Coven
Annie's Room
The Ash House
Asylum
B&B
The Bride of Ashbyrn House
The Camera Man
The Curse of Wetherley House
The Devil, the Witch and the Whore
Devil's Briar
The Dog
Eli's Town
The Farm
The Ghost of Molly Holt
The Ghosts of Lakeforth Hotel
The Girl Who Never Came Back
Haunted
The Haunting of Blackwych Grange
Like Stones on a Crow's Back
The Night Girl
Perfect Little Monsters & Other Stories
Stephen
The Shades
The Soul Auction
Tenderling
Ward Z

ESCAPE FROM HOTEL NECRO

AMY CROSS

This edition
first published by Dark Season Books,
United Kingdom, 2019

ISBN: 9781698682075

Also available in e-book format.

www.amycross.com

CONTENTS

Prologue
PAGE 17

Chapter One
PAGE 21

Chapter Two
PAGE 25

Chapter Three
PAGE 29

Chapter Four
PAGE 35

Chapter Five
PAGE 37

Chapter Six
PAGE 41

Chapter Seven
PAGE 45

Chapter Eight
PAGE 47

Chapter Nine
PAGE 51

Chapter Ten
PAGE 59

Chapter Eleven
page 63

Chapter Twelve
page 65

Chapter Thirteen
page 67

Chapter Fourteen
page 69

Chapter Fifteen
page 79

Chapter Sixteen
page 85

Chapter Seventeen
page 89

Chapter Eighteen
page 95

Chapter Nineteen
page 99

Chapter Twenty
page 103

Chapter Twenty-one
page 111

Chapter Twenty-two
PAGE 115

Chapter Twenty-three
PAGE 117

Chapter Twenty-four
PAGE 119

Chapter Twenty-five
PAGE 121

Chapter Twenty-six
PAGE 129

Chapter Twenty-seven
PAGE 137

Chapter Twenty-eight
PAGE 143

Chapter Twenty-nine
PAGE 151

Chapter Thirty
PAGE 159

Chapter Thirty-one
PAGE 165

Chapter Thirty-two
PAGE 169

CHAPTER THIRTY-THREE
PAGE 179

CHAPTER THIRTY-FOUR
PAGE 185

CHAPTER THIRTY-FIVE
PAGE 191

CHAPTER THIRTY-SIX
PAGE 199

CHAPTER THIRTY-SEVEN
PAGE 207

CHAPTER THIRTY-EIGHT
PAGE 213

CHAPTER THIRTY-NINE
PAGE 225

CHAPTER FORTY
PAGE 229

EPILOGUE
PAGE 237

ESCAPE FROM HOTEL NECRO

PROLOGUE

I MAKE MY WAY across the room, while keeping my gaze fixed on her terrified stare. She starts shaking violently again, more violently with each step that I take toward her. I feel more powerful than I've ever felt before in my life, and as I stop and stare down at her face I realize that there's nothing holding me back. I can slash and rip and burn, I can tear her to pieces, and I don't even have to care.

Reaching down, I run a finger's edge across her belly, up over her breasts and then onto her neck. As I move my finger to her jaw, she lets out an anguished, muffled whimper and turns her head away, as if she thinks that can somehow save her.

As if she thinks I might suddenly change my mind.

"I want a razor-blade," I say finally, causing the girl to struggle yet once more against her restraints. "It doesn't have to be big. In fact, I think a smaller one might be better. I can be more... accurate."

I run my finger up the side of her face as tears run down her cheeks.

A moment later, I feel a nice, small razor-blade being placed in my right hand, and I hold it up for her to see.

She struggles again, with such force this time that the chair seems to be at risk of coming loose from its bolts.

"This is going to hurt," I explain, "and it's going to last for as long as possible. But that won't be any fun if you still have that thing in your mouth."

Reaching around, I loosen the knot at the back of her head, and then I pull the gag away.

"Help me!" she screams, as blood sprays from her mouth. "Somebody help me!"

"Who do you think is coming?" I ask calmly, as I turn the razor-blade around between my fingers. "There's no-one out there. No-one cares. But don't worry, I'll save your eyes for last. I want to see them as I'm doing all the other things."

I hold the razor-blade out and set its edge against her left nipple.

"I'll kill you!" she snarls, pulling harder than

ever against the restraints. “When I get out of here, I'll kill you!”

“You won't be getting out of here,” I reply, with the faintest twitch of a smile. “Didn't you realize that yet? You have no chance of leaving this place.” I lean closer to her. “Welcome to Hotel Necro!”

ONE

Two days earlier...

"HOW DO YOU SLEEP at night?"

As I grab my suitcase from the back of the taxi, I feel Jason's hands on the sides of my waist.

"Seriously," he continues, "you're so hot, you should be illegal. How do you sleep, knowing that you're such a total babe?"

I set the suitcase down and turn to him, and then I raise a skeptical eyebrow. He's so cute and so sweet, and sometimes he goes *way* overboard.

"When I get you into this hotel room," he says with a sly grin, "I'm going to -"

"You're going to take a shower," I tell him, "because that two hour flight did you no favors in the under-arm department. If you know what I mean."

Furrowing his brow, he sniffs his left armpit.

"I smell fine," he says plaintively. "Don't I?"

"You smell lovely," I tell him, "but you could smell... less."

He sniffs his other armpit.

"It's nothing," he says. "I smell great. Anyway, I'm only going to work up a sweat with you later."

"I appreciate the comments," I continue, "but you're trying just a little bit too much." Reaching up, I touch the scar in the left side of my cheek, and I can still feel the rippled edges of skin that had to be sewn back together after the accident. Incident. Whatever. "I meant what I said the other day. I'm not having some kind of crisis of confidence about my looks. It's only a small scar, and it doesn't bother me."

He smiles.

"I'm more concerned about this hotel you booked," I add, grabbing the handle of my suitcase and looking past Jason. "Hotel Necro? Is that seriously its name?"

"What's wrong with that?" he asks as he hands some money to the taxi driver. "Necro's pretty cool, right? I think it's something to do with magic. We're gonna create a *lot* of magic ourselves this weekend. Between the sheets, if you know what I mean."

"I'm pretty sure Necro refers to death."

"Huh?"

"Necro relates to death," I say again, before leaning closer and giving him a peck on the cheek. "But don't worry about it, Jason. The name probably just got lost in translation, and it *does* look like a nice hotel. Actually, it looks *really* nice. Are you sure we can afford something this classy?"

He steps around and puts his arms around me, hugging me tight. As he does that, the taxi pulls away.

"Nothing's too good for you," he says, as he kisses the side of my neck. "After everything that happened to you, you deserve a chance to rest and relax. Despite the slightly odd name, Hotel Necro is one of the most popular and exclusive boutique luxury hotels in the whole of Turin, and you're going to have the best weekend of your life. And that's an order."

Smiling, I realize once again that I'm so lucky to have Jason. Without him, I don't know how I'd ever have managed to get through the past few weeks. Getting out of New York was probably a really good idea.

"You need this," he continues, before kissing the other side of my neck. "We both do. We need this vacation, or we're gonna go crazy."

TWO

"AND MISS CATHERINE JOHNSON," the receptionist says as he takes a look at my passport. "Welcome to Turin, Ms. Johnson, and welcome to Hotel Necro."

"Thanks," I reply with a smile, although deep down I can't help wondering what he's thinking.

He must have noticed the scar. After all, I don't have it in my passport photo, but it's kind of hard to miss the mark on my cheek. The e-passport gate at the airport spat me back, and the guy on the desk there seemed a little embarrassed. I knew exactly what *he* was thinking. Now this receptionist, whose name badge declares him to be called Henri, isn't doing a very good job of hiding his thoughts. In fact, he's kinda staring.

“Is everything okay?” Jason asks.

“Of course, Sir,” Henri replies, setting the passport down and starting to type on his keyboard. “I'll see if it's possible to find you a free upgrade for your stay.”

Jason glances at me, and I can see from the look in his eyes that he noticed what just happened. I just hope he doesn't say anything. Sometimes he tries way too hard to be chivalrous and protective. I'd rather just get to the room.

“This place looks really lovely,” I say, hoping to lighten the mood a little and change the subject. “I never saw it mentioned in any of the guides to Turin. You've got a nice little secret hotel hidden away here.”

Henri glances at me and smiles, but he quickly gets back to his work on the computer. Great, now he seems to not want to look at me at all. I'm not sure what's worse.

Behind, Jason's hand slides onto my butt, but I quickly reach back and ease the hand away. I love him for everything he's done lately, but he's trying a little too hard to make me feel that I'm still attractive. As I look at the mirror on the facing wall, I see my reflection staring back and I tell myself that the scar really isn't *that* bad. It's fairly fresh, too, which means that it still has time to heal some more. Maybe one day, with a little make-up, it'll barely be visible at all.

"I have for you the perfect room," Henri announces, as he takes a plastic key-card and places it on the sensor. "In fact, you're in luck. I can put you in the best room in the entire hotel, all for no extra charge."

"See?" Jason says, nudging me with his hip. "That's a good omen. It shows that things are finally looking up. The world's on our side again."

THREE

"WOW, LOOK AT THIS room!" Jason calls out as he makes his way toward the windows and looks out across the city. "Are you kidding? How good is this? I've never stayed anywhere so cool in my whole life!"

"It's certainly swanky," I reply, setting my suitcase down and then letting the door gently swing shut. "I know I shouldn't keep asking, but... Are you *sure* we can afford this place?"

"I told you, everything's covered." He turns to me, and he hesitates for a moment. "Did you take your pills, honey?"

I nod.

"Are you sure?"

"Yes."

I unzip my suitcase.

“I didn't see you do it,” he adds.

“I did it on the plane,” I reply, glancing at him. “Relax.”

I start rooting through my case, hoping to find a few of the dresses that I packed for the weekend. I was expecting sunny weather, but now there's a forecast of rain possibly arriving on Sunday.

“Maybe you should put your pills out in the bathroom,” Jason says after a moment, “so you know you won't forget to take them at the proper times.”

“I won't forget.”

“It might be good to just... make sure.”

“I haven't forgotten to take one so far,” I reply, trying to hide the fact that I'm slightly annoyed. After all, I'm a grown woman, I can be trusted to take my medication. “Besides,” I add, “I have *you* to remind me. And you're being very careful to do that twice a day, right on schedule.”

“It's only because I love you,” he points out. “I just want you to be okay.”

“I'm better than okay,” I reply, as I hold up two dresses for him to see. “Now, onto more important matters. We're eating here at the hotel tonight, right? So which one of these do you think fits in better with the decor of the magnificent Hotel Necro?”

“You're so beautiful,” he says.

"Look at the dresses, Casanova," I say firmly. "Which one would you like me to wear for dinner?"

FOUR

"YOU LOOK ABSOLUTELY STUNNING," Jason says as we sit at a table in a corner of the hotel's restaurant. We're the only diners here so far, and classical music is being piped into the room. "I'm the luckiest guy in the world."

"Scallop sashimi," I say, focusing on the menu and trying to change the subject a little. "Have I had that before?"

"Not with me."

"I don't remember ever having it," I reply, "but it seems familiar somehow." I pause for a moment, and I quickly realize that there's a strange sensation in my mouth. "It's like I can somehow remember the taste, even though I don't think I've ever eaten it. Is that weird?"

"I don't know." He hesitates. "Not really. I

guess. Maybe. I guess memories are pretty weird. But hey, why not have the duck egg as a starter instead?"

"I love duck eggs," I reply, "but I'm kinda curious about this scallop sashimi. I think I want to try that for a change."

"Why not just stick with an old favorite?" he asks.

"We're on vacation. Isn't it good to try new things?"

"It's good to have things you like, too."

I hesitate, before realizing that maybe he's right. This is a fancy restaurant and I should just go with a fancy version of something I know I like. It's a good job Jason thought about that, otherwise I might have ended up sitting here with twenty euros of cold seafood that I don't even like.

"There's that look in your eyes again," he says suddenly.

I look at him.

"Like you're a million miles away," he continues. "You know, sometimes I really wonder what's going on in that head of yours. You just seem like you're in another world, like there's a part of you that's always... away, somehow."

"I'm not away anywhere," I reply, suddenly feeling guilty. I reach across the table and touch his right hand. "I'm right here. With you, which is the only place I want to be in the whole world."

He smiles, and I think I might have managed to get through to him.

“I'll prove it to you later,” I continue, squeezing his hand slightly. “I promise.”

FIVE

HE LETS OUT A gasp as he finishes. He explodes inside me, and I squeeze his shoulders tight and feel the muscles contract. There's a moment of absolutely stillness, as if the wheels of the universe have briefly stopped turning, and then slowly he slides himself out and rolls onto his back.

"That was amazing," he says breathlessly, staring up at the ceiling. "That felt so good, like... I don't know, it was just the best ever."

"Totally," I reply, as I close my legs and pull the ruffled sheets over my naked body.

"It was good for you too, right?"

"Of course."

"Did you finish?"

"Yeah," I reply, but I already know that I sound less than convincing. I turn to him. "It's not only about the climax," I add. "I don't *always* have to have an orgasm. Sometimes I like just... feeling you inside."

He stares at me, as if he's a little disappointed that he couldn't make me finish. I know that expression so well. For the longest time now, I've struggled to be everything he wants in bed. I've tried to fake the pleasure, and that was a complete disaster. Now it seems that being honest isn't working too well either.

"Next time," I continue, reaching up and touching his right hand, and slipping my fingers between his. "You know I have trouble getting to that point, but I really enjoy trying. Like, a lot."

He pauses, and then he smiles before leaning over and kissing me on the cheek. I know he's not entirely happy, but we've had this conversation so many times before. These new pills are having a few unexpected side effects, one of which is that I just can't seem to climax during intercourse. Jason says he understands but, once again, I know that deep down he feels like a failure. I guess that's natural. It doesn't matter how many times I try to convince him otherwise: he feels as if he's not satisfying me.

"I just want you to be happy," he says finally, still trying to get his breath back. "That's all. In every way, too. Emotionally. Intellectually. Physically."

"And I am," I tell him. "Honestly. You don't need to keep checking."

"Annoying, huh?"

"Sweet," I reply, before giving him a peck on the cheek, "but unnecessary. And now, if you'll excuse me, I need to take a little trip to the bathroom."

"Don't forget your pills," he says as I climb out of bed. "I took the liberty of setting them out next to the sink."

"Thanks," I reply, stifling the urge to tell him that I really don't need the help. "That's so sweet of you."

SIX

I LOOK SO DIFFERENT in the bathroom's stark electric light. Older, somehow, and a little sickly. I know that's mainly due to the bulbs they use, but for a moment I can only stare at my face and wonder whether it's really me staring back.

I manage a faint smile.

My reflection does the same.

Reaching behind my head, I gather my hair into a bunch and then I slip a hairband into place. Jason keeps telling me how much he likes it when I wear my hair down, but I think maybe I'd like to have it up tomorrow. Just for a change. I don't mean to get all vain, but I think having my hair up suits my face a little better. It makes me look a little smarter, a little more switched on. More modern.

Okay, maybe I'm being *slightly* vain, but is

that really the biggest sin in the world? And it's not as if I'm hung up on my scar. I swear, I'm almost getting used to the damn thing.

Once I've made sure that the hairband is in place, I finish tying the front of my hotel-issued gown. I'm about to go back through into the room when I spot my two red pills resting on the side, waiting for me. There's the round red pill that's designed to help me sleep, and there's the oblong red pill that helps me stay calm. I hesitate, briefly considering the option of keeping my head and body clear by skipping the pills, but then I realize that I have no choice. I need my medication, so I take the pills and chase them down with a glass of water.

"I'm so tired," I say to Jason as I head into the main room and make my way to the bed. "I don't think I'll have any -"

"What did you do that for?" he asks, suddenly sitting up and looking worried.

"Do what?"

"Your hair." He stares at me for a moment, as if I've done something utterly astonishing.

"I just thought I'd try it out for tomorrow," I reply, surprised by his reaction. "Why? Don't you like it?"

"You look beautiful, as ever," he says cautiously, "but... I don't know, I just think I like it more when it's down."

“Does it matter for one day?” I ask. “We're only going to be out sight-seeing. It's not like it's really important.”

“Sure,” he replies, but I can tell that he's still not convinced. For some reason, he seems *really* hung up on this hair thing. “It's totally your choice, Katie. I just...”

His voice trails off.

“You know what?” I reply, before reaching back and pulling the band away, letting my hair fall back down to my shoulders. “It doesn't really matter either way. Is that better?”

“Much,” he says, smiling a smile of palpable relief. “I just think you'll feel more comfortable like that, Katie. You know, in the hot weather. Tomorrow's supposed to be *really* hot.”

“Really?” I slip out of the gown and climb into bed. “I thought I saw a forecast for rain.”

“I won't *let* it rain,” he replies as I settle down. “I refuse to let the weather be anything other than perfect. There's going to be gorgeous sunshine, and we'll have the most brilliant day ever.”

“I'm sure we will,” I reply, kissing him on the cheek before setting my head on the pillow. Suddenly I feel really tired, as if I can barely keep my eyes open. “Do you mind turning off the light, honey?” I ask, letting my lids slip shut. “I don't know what's come over me, I think it's just all the traveling, I think...”

My voice trails off, and I can feel myself falling asleep already. I hear a clicking sound and the room falls dark, and then I feel the bed shift beneath me as Jason rolls onto his side. I'm already half asleep, and I don't fight as I feel myself sinking deeper and deeper into rest. After the long flight today, I need this so bad. Maybe I'm suffering from a little jet-lag, too. I just want to sleep and sleep and sleep and wake up in the morning feeling rested and ready to go.

I just want to enjoy this vacation.

SEVEN

BLOOD SPRAYS EVERYWHERE, splattering against my face and into my mouth as I laugh.

EIGHT

SUDDENLY I OPEN MY eyes and see a crack of morning light running across the ceiling. I stay completely still for a moment, listening to the beautiful silence, and then I start to sit up. Immediately, however, I feel an instant sense of panic in my chest. My heart is racing and I'm filled with the sense that something's wrong.

I try again to sit up, but this time I feel a sharp pain in my left side, at the bottom of my ribs.

Letting the sheet fall down, I see that there's a bruise on my side, along with a small scratch.

"What the..."

I touch the bruise and feel an instant tremor of pain, and a moment later I hear Jason rolling over next to me.

"Are you okay?" he asks.

"Yeah," I reply, as I touch the bruise again, "it's just... Look at this."

"You must have bumped yourself."

"In my sleep?"

"I guess." He pauses. "Did you get up to use the bathroom in the night?"

"No," I rcply. "I mean, I don't think so."

"Then maybe you hit it on the edge of the bedside table."

"Seriously? This looks like I got *punched*!"

"I'm pretty sure you didn't get punched," he replies. "Does it hurt?"

"Kinda."

"Much?"

I pause. "No," I admit finally, "but more than it should. There shouldn't be anything there at all!"

"It'll heal in a day or two," he replies, as he climbs out of bed and walks over to the window. Still naked, he grabs the edges of the drapes and pulls them open, allowing the rest of the morning light to flood into the room. Momentarily blinded, I have to hold a hand up to protect my eyes.

"Look at this place," Jason exclaims, putting his hands on his hips. "We have a whole new city to explore, Katie. What do you say we get some breakfast and then head out? There's no point sitting around in our room when there's so much to do." He turns to me, still with his hands on his hips. "Do you want to shower first?"

"Sure," I reply, as I start to get out of bed. As I do so, however, I feel a surprising soreness in my legs. It's almost as if I just went through leg day at the gym, except I haven't been to the gym all week. "I feel pretty stiff," I continue. "Like I've done a full workout."

"Well," he replies, "we *did* get a little energetic last night."

I can't help but roll my eyes.

"What?" he says with a grin. "You went on top for a while, remember?"

"I think it'd take more than that," I say as I get to my feet and grab the gown, before limping slightly on my way to the bathroom. "I won't be long."

"And don't forget to take your pills," he calls after me.

I stop in the doorway, but I don't turn to him. I don't mean to seem ungrateful, but I really wish he'd stop reminding me over and over about those pills. The more he mentions them, the more I want to skip them, just to be contrary.

"They're very important," he adds. "You really mustn't get out of the habit."

"I won't," I reply, bristling again at the sense that I'm being coddled. Still, Jason's only trying to help out, and it'd be wrong of me to say anything. "Give me five minutes," I add, turning to him and smiling. “I'll be right out.”

Once I'm in the bathroom, I lock the door and head to the sink. Jason has already been through to set out my two red pills for the day, which is very conscientious of him. It's odd, but I hadn't realized that he'd been up already this morning. I guess maybe he put the pills out in the middle of the night.

I start the shower running, and then I head to the mirror and take a closer look at the wound on my side. The bruise is really discolored, with a dark brown center surrounded by reddish and purplish patches and a ring of yellow, while the scratches look quite deep. The skin around the edges is slightly inflamed, and I really don't understand how I could have suffered an injury like this while I was asleep.

Then again, it's not like anything else could have happened, so I guess this must just have been some freak injury.

“Damn it,” I mutter as I touch the bruise again, “that really hurts.”

I guess I should stop poking it.

NINE

"WOW, THIS PLACE IS busy," I say a while later, as Jason and I try to squeeze our way along a packed street. "I can barely move. It's like we're walking in a perpetual queue."

"And this is *outside* of the usual tourist season," he replies. "Imagine what it must be like when it's *really* busy."

"Can we take a side street?" I ask.

"We'll be fine, it's not much further to the cathedral."

"Sure," I reply, before grabbing his hand and leading him into a narrow, cobbled street that leads off the main area, "but at least down here we can breathe." I take a deep breath, as if to prove my point. "I swear, I was going crazy out there. Sometimes, when there are so many people all around, I just feel like I'm getting a little light-headed."

"You might have a point," he says, although he seems a little uncertain as he takes his phone from his pocket and brings up a map. "Come on, it won't make much difference if we go this way. And I guess we're getting to see a quieter, more authentic part of town."

He's not wrong about that. In fact, as we make our way along the gloomy street, I can't help looking up and seeing scores of lines running between the buildings on either side. The lines are covered in clothes that have been hung out to dry, and a moment later I spot a woman glaring at us from one of the high windows. I smile, but she quickly pulls back inside and closes her shutters.

Somewhere nearby, a dog is barking.

"Well, it's quaint," I say, hoping to keep our spirits up as we cross an intersection. "I'll give it that. It smells a little..."

"Authentic?" Jason suggests.

"Exactly. It smells authentic. That's the polite word." We take a left and head along another street. "Maybe a little *too* authentic. Honey, are you sure we're going in the right direction? I feel like we're heading more *away* from the cathedral."

"No, this is definitely the way," he says, before stopping suddenly and peering more closely at his phone's screen. "Of course, I don't really have good signal down here, probably because the walls are so high." He holds his phone up and waits to see if his signal will improve. "It's like a maze in these streets. Maybe you were right, maybe we should've just stuck with the main drag after all."

"I'm sure we can find our way," I tell him.

"Wait right here," he adds, turning and heading back the way we just came.

"Where are you going?"

"I had signal back around that corner," he explains. "I just need to check a map."

"I'll come with you."

"No, wait there." He glances back at me. "I'll be thirty seconds, I promise."

I open my mouth to ask why I can't just go with him, but he quickly disappears around the corner and I realize that there's no point arguing with him. Jason always likes to take charge of situations, and sometimes he can get a little hurt if I don't let him. I could do without being left standing here like a total idiot, but I'm sure he'll be back just as soon as he's managed to check a map.

Sighing, I turn and take a few more steps along the street, while looking up at the clothes lines that are fluttering high above me. This place definitely has its own charm, and I guess it's good to get away from the tourist areas a little. It's so easy to end up shuffling from one iconic location to another, without really seeing anything of the real life in a place like this. For a moment, I feel utterly at peace, and I realize after a few seconds that there's a faint smile on my face.

Suddenly a voice says something in Italian.

Startled, I look around, but it takes a moment before I see the girl sitting cross-legged in a nearby doorway. She's wearing a black coat and a pale blue hoodie, and she must be in her early twenties. She's staring at me with dark, frantic eyes.

"English?" she continues, as she holds out her right hand and shows me the palm. "Money."

"I'm sorry," I reply, a little taken aback, "I don't have any."

"Money."

"I'm sorry, I -"

"Money."

"I really don't have any," I say, forcing a smile. "I'm sorry. Have a nice day."

With that, I turn to go back and find Jason. After just a single step, however, I hear a rustling sound over my shoulder and I realize that the girl must have stood up. I hesitate, worried that she might get funny with me, but then I tell myself that I just need to keep walking and -

Suddenly I'm shoved from behind and sent slamming against the wall, and then I feel the girl press her arm against the back of my neck.

"Money," she sneers into my ear, before turning me around and holding up a screwdriver.

"Money."

"I don't have any money to give you," I stammer, as I realize that I'm being mugged. "I swear!"

"Money." She leans closer. "Any money. Euros. Pounds. Dollar. Anything."

"I don't have any. I only -"

Before I can finish, she shoves the screwdriver's tip down against my belly and pushes hard. I instinctively let out a gasp as I feel a flash of pain.

"Don't hurt me!" I stammer.

"Money," she snarls again, as she starts twisting the screwdriver and pushing harder. She must be close to driving it straight into my stomach.

"I don't have any!" I tell her. "You can have anything you want, anything I've got, but I don't have any money! Take my purse! Take all of it, but you'll see for yourself! I don't have any money to give you!"

She stares at me with an expression of pure anger, as if she doesn't believe me.

"You give me money," she says finally. "Now."

"Please," I reply, desperately trying to work out how I'm going to get out of this situation, "I -"

"Money!"

She rams the screwdriver harder against my belly, and at the same time she twists the handle.

The pain is instant and strong, and I grit my teeth as I put my hands on the woman's chest and try to push her away.

"What don't you understand?" she hisses. "I need money! Now!"

"I don't have any money," I tell her yet again, and now my voice is trembling with fear. "Please, if you don't believe me, check for yourself. Take my bag! I don't -"

She digs the screwdriver deeper, and I let out an involuntary cry.

"Hey!" Jason shouts suddenly in the distance. "What are you doing?"

Turning, I see to my relief that he's rushing this way. I look back at the girl and see pure fury in her eyes.

Suddenly she spits in my face. I turn away, and in that moment she pulls back and runs. I immediately slide down to the ground and start wiping the thick, slimy mucus from my eyes and nose, while Jason reaches me and crouches down.

"Are you okay?" he asks frantically. "Katie, talk to me!"

"I think so," I stammer, as I sniff back tears and lift the bottom of my shirt to reveal a reddened but somehow not broken patch of skin where the screwdriver pressed against me. The tip didn't pierce my skin after all. "She wanted money."

"I should never have left you here!" he says

firmly, pulling me close and giving me a big hug. “This was all my fault.”

“It wasn't your fault,” I whimper, but I start to sob as I press my face against his shoulder. I try to tell him again that he mustn't blame himself, but I can't get the words out and soon I'm a blubbering mess. I guess it's just the shock of being attacked in broad daylight.

“I'll never leave you alone like that again,” Jason says firmly, holding me tight. “I promise.”

TEN

"REALLY, I'M FINE," I say as we sit in a cafe near one of the main tourist squares. "It was just a fright, that's all. There's no harm done."

"If I ever see that girl again," he replies angrily, "I'll -"

"It's over," I add, cutting him off. I reach out and hold his hand. "You won't see her again. I mean, come on, how many people live in Turin? Besides, no-one was hurt, not in the end. I didn't even get so much as a scratch."

"I bet she lives down that street," he mutters. "I should go back there later and find her, and -"

"No!"

He sighs and leans back in his seat.

"Maybe I should file a police report,

though," I tell him. "They might be able to do something."

"They won't give a damn," he says.

"But if -"

"They won't care, Katie," he says firmly. "They'll waste our time asking for a statement, and then they'll throw all the paperwork in the bin. The police aren't the answer to kids like that. What that girl needs is a lesson she'll never forget. She needs some good old-fashioned discipline."

"I'm fine," I say, before noticing a couple sitting at another table. The woman – who happens to have an old-fashioned beehive hairstyle – is staring at me, although she quickly looks away. "Ignore the fact that I cried," I continue, turning back to Jason. "That was just caused by shock."

I wait for him to reply, but after a moment I realize that Beehive Lady is looking at me again. I try to ignore her, even though I'm sure I've seen her somewhere before. I guess she and her husband – who has an impossibly chiseled jaw – might also be staying at Hotel Necro, although after a moment I see from the corner of my eye that the woman is tapping at her phone. After a moment, she turns the phone to show her husband whatever's on the screen.

"I'd never forgive myself if something happened to you," Jason says sternly.

"That's very sweet and heroic," I tell him,

hoping that I can calm him down. “You're my knight in shining armor.” Realizing that I might have accidentally sounded sarcastic, I give his hand another squeeze. “Stuff happens,” I remind him. “Come on, let's not let this ruin our trip.”

“I just want to find the little bitch and throttle her.”

“Now that really *would* ruin our day,” I point out.

As I say those words, I see that Beehive Lady on the other table is still showing her phone to her husband. After a moment, Chisel Jaw turns and looks at me, but then they both pretend that they're looking at something else. A moment later they both turn away, although I have no doubt that – for some reason – *I* was the object of their attention. They weren't very good at hiding their interest.

“I know you're right,” Jason says after a few seconds. “I just hate that bad things happen to good people. The world shouldn't be like that.”

“Things aren't so bad,” I tell him. I glance at the other couple for a moment, but they seem to have finally stopped watching me. “There are a few bad apples, but most people are good. And some, like you...” I pause, and finally I smile at him. “Some, like you, are exceptional. And I'm fully aware that I'm the luckiest woman in the whole world.”

ELEVEN

"KATIE, ARE YOU COMING?"

"Just a moment," I reply, as I stand in the bathroom and stare at the pills in the palm of my hand. I've been doing this for several minutes now, and I still can't make up my mind.

If I take the pills, I'll be obeying my doctor's instructions. I'll be being a good patient. But I'll also messing with my body, and that has consequences. For once, I want to actually give Jason what he wants in bed, and I figure there can't be *that* much harm in skipping a single dose. I'll get right back on the pills in the morning, and no-one will ever know that I did anything wrong. I mean, there's some logic to that plan, right?

I swallow the oblong pill, but then I slip the round pill into my toiletry bag. I'm pretty sure that's the pill that's been causing me problems in the bedroom, and I'm willing to give it a miss for just one night. Jason would be furious if he found out, but he *won't* find out.

"Katie?"

"On my way," I reply, turning and heading out of the bathroom. I guess there's no turning back now.

TWELVE

I CRY OUT AS the wave of pleasure hits my body, and as the pleasure finally explodes and I climax for the first time in months. I pull Jason tight, almost as if I'm trying to pull his entire body into mine, and I press my crotch against him as tight as I can manage. I want the moment to last forever, and for a few seconds I feel as if it might. Finally, however, the intense ecstasy starts to fade, and I'm left panting breathlessly and still squeezing Jason so that I can enjoy the full comedown from that amazing high.

"Wow," Jason says finally, "did you..."

His voice trails off.

"Oh yeah," I gasp. "Couldn't you tell?"

"Sure, I just..."

I look up at him, and I can see the confusion

in his eyes. At the same time, there's a faint smile on his lips, and he's starting to look pretty pleased with himself. In any other situation, he'd be suspicious, but... Well, I love Jason very much, and I guess he's too relieved to really question how I did what I did.

"I told you it'd happen if we just stopped stressing about it," I remind him. "You didn't ever doubt me, did you?"

"Of course not," he replies, although he's clearly still a little shocked. "I mean, no, never. I guess I just wasn't expecting it. It kind of... came out of the blue."

"I aim to surprise," I say, reaching up and gently moving some sweaty hair from across his forehead. "You know I love you, don't you?"

"I love you so much," he says, and then he starts kissing me gently.

He's still inside me as I pull him tight, and as the kiss continues. I feel a little guilty for not having told him exactly *how* I managed to achieve an orgasm tonight, but I guess the ends justify the means. He's clearly so happy that we both climaxed, and it feels good to have avoided the usual faint air of being a letdown. Although I have to admit that I'm once again starting to feel exhausted.

I think I'm going to sleep *very* well tonight.

THIRTEEN

"OKAY," A VOICE SAYS in the distance, breaking through the haze of sleep, "are you ready? Lift on my mark. One. Two. Three."

FOURTEEN

MY EYES BLINK OPEN, just as a long electric strip light passes my field of vision from top to bottom and then disappears from view. Beneath me, some kind of metal trolley bumps slightly over an uneven floor.

"So then I told them," a man's voice says nearby, "I just want to transfer to some other role. Anything'll do, I just want a challenge. Like, a proper challenge. Not one of those fake challenges that people really want when they're just pretending they want a challenge."

Another strip light briefly appears, and I realize that I'm flat on my back and that I'm being wheeled along a corridor. I try to blink, but now I find that I can't even move my eyelids. My first thought is that I must be in a hospital, that something awful must have happened, but after a moment I realize that the ceiling above me looks strangely grubby and dark, and low too. What kind of hospital looks like that?

"What did they say?" another man asks.

"What do you *think* they said?" The first man sighs. "They don't give a damn. Eventually I just backed off and decided to stick with what I've got now. And that's the whole point, dude. They won't lift a finger to help you, so don't even try. You want to move to another division? Fat chance. You'll stay where they put you and you'll be grateful for that."

Suddenly there's a bumping sound, and I realize I'm being wheeled through a set of open double doors. The trolley shudders slightly as it hits the frame.

I try to open my mouth and ask what's happening, but for some reason I can't seem to move my body at all. I can feel my jaw, but it seems to be far too heavy. I try again and again to make it move, and I can feel my flesh twitching, but it's as if the bone itself is made of lead. Then, when I try to sit up, I find that the rest of my body is the same. I can't move at all. I swear, I feel as if my skeleton has become impossibly heavy and firm, leaving my flesh to struggle vainly in a desperate attempt to move.

"I thought there'd be *some* possibility of

advancement," the second man grumbles as they continue to wheel me along the corridor. "I mean, I think I'm doing a pretty good job. Don't they *want* good workers to stick around? Or are we just totally expendable?"

"We're hired grunts," the first man says firmly, "and don't you forget it. Hold that one open, it's a fire door."

The trolley stops for a moment, and I hear a brief creaking sound before I get going again. Someone grunts nearby, and I suddenly find myself in a room with a much higher ceiling.

"I don't know what it's like where you're from, but back home in Malta there's not much decent work. Not work like this, anyway. That's why I came to Italy."

I try again to move, but I can't so much as turn my head. I can't even blink anymore, and I'm starting to panic as the trolley is swung around and then stopped. A moment later I hear a clicking sound behind my head, and then suddenly a man's face appears directly in front of me, staring straight down into my eyes.

"Ms. Johnson?" he says with an expectant grin. "Wakey wakey. Time for night two."

He waits, and after a moment his grin fades a little.

"Ms. Johnson?"

He hesitates, before turning and looking at

someone I can't see.

"You gave her the jab, right?"

"Of course. Back in their room."

The man looks back down at me, and then he gently taps the side of my face. I can feel the tapping sensation, even though I still can't move even one inch of my body.

"Ms. Sinclair," he says firmly, "this is Doctor Strickland. Can you hear me? Ms. Sinclair, if you can hear me, I need you to give me a sign. Anything."

I try to cry out, but again I can't move a muscle. I'm starting to really panic now, to think that I *have* been in an accident. What if I'm badly hurt? What if I'm paralyzed? And what about Jason? Where's my husband?

This Doctor Strickland guy watches me for a moment longer, and then he places two fingers against the side of my neck, as if he's checking for a pulse. He seems increasingly worried.

"What's wrong?" one of the other voices asks. "We did exactly what you told us. We did it the same as we always do. If it isn't working, that's not our fault!"

"She doesn't seem to be responding this time," the man murmurs. "That's odd. She was fine last night, she was a perfect specimen. You saw that for yourselves."

He briefly disappears from view, before

returning with a bright light which he shines straight into my left eye.

I try to cry out, to ask what's happening, but I still can't move my mouth. Even my tongue feels heavy, as if it's made of lead.

The man shines the light into my other eye. The brightness is uncomfortable, but now I can't even blink.

"I don't understand at all," he says finally, as he sets the light aside and furrows his brow. "If she's taken the right pills, which she has, she should be responding by now. She should be up and about, and ready to get started." He turns and looks over his shoulder. "Please don't take this as me doubting you, gentlemen, but would you mind showing me precisely *where* you administered the injection?"

I hear a labored sigh, and then a finger touches my left leg.

I try to flinch and pull away, with no luck.

Another finger touches the leg.

Am I naked?

"Okay," the man says, "I see the two puncture marks. One from last night, and then this fresher one must be tonight's. I can only assume that this is some freak result." He leans over me again. "I'm reluctant to administer another dose, in case there are complications. The precise quantities are carefully regulated, based on factors such as body mass and age. Can someone please go and fetch her husband? I believe he got started early, in room five."

I hear footsteps walking calmly away, as the man continues to peer into my eyes.

"The lights are on," he mutters, "but nobody's home, are they? I'm dreadfully sorry, Ms. Johnson, but on this occasion we seem to have failed you. On behalf of everyone at Hotel Necro, I can only offer my profuse apologies. And I promise, I will get to the bottom of this mishap."

Suddenly there's the sound of someone screaming in the distance. It's a woman, I think, and she seems to be in absolute agony. Doctor Strickland, however, doesn't react at all, and instead he seems more interested in examining me. Was the scream real? Did he hear it? Or was it somehow just in my head?

"This has never happened before," he continues finally, clearly mystified. "I don't like it when my process throws up unexpected results like this. I don't like not knowing why something is happening." He leans even closer to my face, until I can feel his breath. "Ms. Johnson," he whispers, "are you in there? If you can hear me, give me a sign."

I try to scream at him. I strain every sinew in an attempt to let out even the faintest of murmurs. Nothing comes. He must be able to see what I'm doing, however. I'm pushing so hard, I find it impossible to believe that there's no sign somewhere on my face. With all this effort, and I not managing to move at all?

Sighing, he steps back, just as more footsteps enter the room.

"What's going on?" a familiar voice asks. "What's wrong with Katie?"

It's Jason!

He's here!"

"There's nothing to worry about," Doctor Strickland replies. "Mr. Johnson, I'm afraid that – for whatever reason – the process has failed us this evening. Due to the sensitive nature of our work here, I'm reluctant to press on and administer another dose, so I'm left with no option but to end your wife's session. Only for tonight, you understand."

"You can't end it!" Jason says angrily. "Do you have any idea how much I paid for this?"

"Suitable recompense will be worked out by the office," Doctor Strickland explains, "but I'm sure you wouldn't want me to jeopardize your wife's health. Mr. Johnson, are you sure that she took all her medication?"

"Of course I'm sure."

"Is there any way she might have missed one or -"

"I made damn sure that she couldn't do that!" Jason says firmly. "I even checked each time.

Don't try blaming us for your failings, Strickland. If your so-called process hasn't worked tonight, then that's on you and you alone!"

"Mr. Johnson, I -"

Suddenly there's a loud crashing sound, as if something has been shattered.

"Mr. Johnson," Doctor Strickland says calmly, "I understand that you're frustrated, but there's really no need to take your anger out on my equipment. I am very sorry, but your wife will be unable to participate in the process tonight. However, you are of course most welcome to continue. We have plenty of rooms available all through the night and I'm sure you'll find something that will take your fancy."

"What's the point of me doing it alone?" Jason asks.

"It would be different, of course, but I'm sure that a man of your great intelligence would be able to come up with some... interesting variations."

There's a pause, and then I hear Jason sigh. A moment later, he leans over me and peers into my eyes.

"Jason!" I try to scream. "What's happening? Get me out of here!"

Nothing happens, however. My eyes are stinging from the dust that has fallen on them, and I still can't even blink.

"She's not awake, is she?" Jason asks

cautiously.

"No, she can't be," Doctor Strickland replies, as he too leans into view and stares at me. "She's unconscious, even though her eyes are open. Obviously the pills have only partially worked tonight, which is why I was wondering whether there's a possibility that she could have missed one. I'd still like you to double-check that there aren't any pills left in the bathroom, but I suppose it's also possible that one of the pills was faulty in some manner. I'll have the batch double-checked."

"This is completely unacceptable," Jason snaps, looking over at him.

"I agree," Doctor Strickland says, still staring down at me, "but I can assure you of two things, Mr. Johnson. First, this will not happen again. Your third night will go like clockwork. And second..." He leans even closer to me. "I assure you, I *will* find out what caused this to happen tonight."

FIFTEEN

"WHAT?"

Startled, I open my eyes and sit up in bed, and for a moment I feel completely confused. I barely even remember who I am, and it takes a moment before I realize that I'm at the hotel with Jason. My breathing is rapid and frantic, and when I touch the side of my face I find that I'm sweating profusely. After a moment, my fingertips brush against my scar.

Next to me, Jason rolls over.

"Honey?" he says groggily. "Are you okay there?"

I hesitate, before turning to him. A crack of morning light is breaking through the gap in the drapes, and I can just about make out Jason's confused face staring up at me.

"What's wrong?" he continues. "Did you have a nightmare?"

"A..."

I pause for a moment as I try to remember the crazy dream that woke me up. As the seconds pass, fragments of the dream fall back into my thoughts, although it's not easy to figure out exactly how they all fit together. I'm getting flashes of images, of people leaning over me and talking, and after a moment I remember how it felt to be completely paralyzed. I was trying to move and I couldn't budge an inch. There's something else, too. I was scared.

"Katie?" Jason says. "What is it?"

Suddenly he touches me on the shoulder, and I instinctively let out a shocked gasp and turn to him.

"You're trembling," he continues, sitting up in bed. He puts a hand on my shoulder, and this time – although I feel sore and achey all over – I don't pull away. "You're not sick, are you?" he asks, moving his hand up and touching my forehead as if he's checking that I don't have a fever. "You seem kind of cold and clammy."

"I..."

Again, my voice trails off as I stare at him. My mind is racing and I can't quite work out what's happening, although already that crazy dream is starting to fade a little in my thoughts. Some of the details are becoming less distinct, and after a moment I realize that it really *was* just a dream. I force a smile and run a hand through my messy hair, and I tell myself that I'm just being an idiot. It was just a very real, very freaky dream, the details of which are fading with each passing second.

"It's nothing," I say finally. "You were right, I just had a bad dream."

"What was it about?"

"I... Nothing," I lie, figuring that there's no point troubling him with the full nitty gritty. I force a smile, hoping to put him at ease. "I don't know what's wrong with me, I think maybe I was more exhausted than I realized. Maybe coming here has been my first chance to really relax in ages, and my mind must be..."

Must be what?

Completely loopy?

I already remember very little of the dream, but I think I was tied down and I couldn't move, and people were talking all around me. There was a scream in the distance at one point, and Jason was there, and...

And there's no point going into all these details, because it really was *just* a dream.

"I need to go to the bathroom," I say finally, as I climb out of bed. I immediately feel really stiff in my legs and arms, but I guess I must have simply slept a little funny. Is it possible that, while I was dreaming about being tied down, I was actually struggling a little in real life? "I'll only be a couple of minutes."

I wince a little as I half walk, half limp through to the bathroom. Once I'm in there, I lock the door, and then I head over to the sink. I run some cold water and splash plenty on my face, hoping that I can wake myself up a little. After a moment, however, I suddenly remember one of the voices that I heard in my dream:

"Please don't take this as me doubting you, gentlemen, but would you mind showing me precisely *where* you administered the injection? Okay, I see the two puncture marks. One from last night, and then this fresher one must be tonight's. I can only assume that this is some freak result."

I remember someone touching my left leg.

I hesitate for a moment, before looking down and examining the same spot myself. At first I don't see anything, but after a few seconds I realize that there seem to be two very small needle marks. I turn around to get a better view of that patch of skin, but now the marks aren't there at all. The more I examine my upper left leg, the more I realize that the supposed 'puncture marks' might actually just be spots. It's difficult to be sure, but I'm certainly not convinced that they're anything more sinister.

I mean, they *can't* be needle marks, can they?

The dream was just a dream, and I need to keep my head straight.

"Katie?" Jason calls out from the bedroom. "Don't forget to take your pills while you're in there!"

I freeze for a moment, before opening my toiletry bag and rifling through. Sure enough, the 'spare' pill is right where I left it, so I quickly crouch down and slip it into the drain in the shower, and then I take my pills as normal. I guess it's possible that my crazy dream last night was caused by my failure to take my medication properly, in which case I have no-one to blame but myself. I should have been more responsible, instead of chasing some easy fix for a minor problem.

"Did you hear me?" Jason continues. "Katie? I said -"

"I heard you," I reply. "I took them. I'll be out in a moment."

Taking a deep breath, I look at my reflection in the mirror, and I swear I can see the fear in my eyes. That dream really knocked me for six and left me feeling discombobulated, but I know that I need to pull myself together so that I'm good company for Jason. After all, we've already reached the final full day of our stay here in Italy, and the last thing I want is to ruin things for my husband. He put so much care into planning this trip, and I know he pushed the boat out when he booked this fancy

Hotel Necro place. I take another deep breath, and then another, and I tell myself that I have to be strong. If not for myself, then for Jason.

I can't let a stupid dream derail everything.

SIXTEEN

"SO I THOUGHT WE should go and see the castle first," Jason continues as we sit at the breakfast table, "and then do the arcade, because that way we don't have to walk *up* all those steps. I mean, we could do it the other way around, but I don't really fancy that kind of a trek. I don't think my calf muscles would survive."

The couple from the cafe yesterday- Beehive Lady and Chisel Jaw – are at one of the other tables, and I swear they're still watching me. Every time I look over, one of them is staring at me; they turn away quickly enough, but it's very obvious that for some reason they find me very interesting.

"Katie?"

Turning to Jason, I realize that I'm being rude.

"Sure," I say, trying to act as if I heard he was saying. "Whatever you think."

"Or we could just take a rest day," he says cautiously. "If you're not feeling up to doing a lot, we can totally just chill at the hotel or -"

"No, it's fine," I reply, still keeping an eye on the other couple. I watch Beehive Lady for a moment, and then I lean toward Jason. "The couple on that table keep looking at me," I whisper.

"Maybe it's because you're so -"

"I mean it," I continue, cutting him off before he can deliver another half-baked compliment. "They were doing it yesterday, and they're doing it again today. It's getting kind of creepy."

He turns and glances toward them, but of course this is the one moment when they're *not* looking at me.

"I don't think you have anything to worry about," he says, turning back to me. "They don't look like serial killers to me. They look more like they just stepped out of the page of some 1960's magazine spread about suburban lifestyle choices."

He chuckles.

"I'm sorry," I reply, "I guess I'm just feeling out of sorts today."

"Still thinking about that bad dream, huh? What happened in it, anyway? You haven't told me all the gory details."

“It doesn't matter.”

“A burden shared is a burden halved.”

“There's really nothing,” I tell him, not really wanting to think about the dream again. “Let's just keep ourselves really busy all day today, yeah? It's our last day in Italy and I don't want to waste it. Let's have some fun!”

SEVENTEEN

"THE HISTORY OF THIS city is insane," Jason explains as we make our way across the hotel lobby, heading out for the day. "I was reading that the -"

"Mr. Johnson?"

We both turn and see that Henri, the man at reception, is gesturing for our attention.

"Mr. Johnson," hc continues as we walk over, "I'm sorry to bother you, but the manager has asked to see you. It won't take long, but would you perhaps mind if I take you through to his office?"

"Uh, sure," Jason says, although he seems a little reluctant. "No problem."

"What's this about?" I ask.

"Everything's fine," Henri says with a broad, well-practiced grin. "Your husband will be back out shortly."

"I'll come with you," I tell Jason.

"No," he says quickly. "I mean, it's fine. I'm sure this is something totally boring. Just wait here for a minute or two, honey, and I'll be straight back out."

He kisses me on the forehead, and then – before I have a chance to argue with him – he heads around the desk and follows Henri through into one of the rear rooms. Sure, Jason can be very old-fashioned when it comes to certain things, but I can't help feeling as if I keep getting pushed to the sidelines.

"Sure," I say, somewhat started by the speed of his departure, "I'll just stand around here and twiddle my thumbs. No problem."

Sighing, I turn and wander over to take a look at a large, oval sculpture that's standing on a table in front of the window. It's kind of an abstract thing, like a large gray egg that got elongated, and I have to admit that I'm not really getting much from it in terms of meaning. I reach out and run my hand across the surface, and I find that it's much smoother than it looks. I've never really been very good when it comes to understanding art, and I have no idea what this sculpture is supposed to 'say'. It's still kind of cool, however, and as I continue to run my hand over its surface I find my mind starting to empty. I guess that meditative quality could, in fact, be the sculpture's purpose all along.

"It's beautiful, isn't it?" a voice says suddenly.

Startled, I turn to find that Beehive Lady is standing just a few feet behind me.

"Sorry," she continues, "I didn't mean to ruin your moment."

"It's fine," I reply, pulling my hand away from the sculpture, "I was just -"

And then it hits me. I know this woman. I don't know how, or where from, or when, but I'm suddenly struck by the overwhelming certainty that we've met before. I don't just mean passing glances in breakfast rooms and cafes, either. I mean, I've *met* her before and *talked* to her. She just suddenly feels... important.

"Are you okay?" she asks.

"I'm fine," I stammer, as I realize that I must have looked like a lunatic while I was staring at her.

"My husband thinks it's about the nature of life and growth," she says, stepping past me and reaching out to touch the sculpture. "He thinks it's a reflection of the fact that we never really emerge from the egg. We *think* we do, but in reality we're always trapped in there, and the world around is us a kind of illusion. No matter hard far we look, we'll never see beyond the inside of our own shell." She runs her hand across the sculpture, and for a moment she seems lost in her own thoughts. "Me?" she adds finally. "I think it's just a big cool shape. I guess I'm a little shallow in that regard."

"I don't really know *what* it's about," I tell her. "I'm not very good at art."

She hesitates, before sliding her hand off the sculpture and holding it out to me.

"Michelle," she says with a faint smile. "Have we met before?"

"I don't think so," I say cautiously, shaking her hand.

"I'm sure I've seen you around," she continues. "Is this your first time here?"

"It is."

"And are you enjoying it?"

Her hand slips away from mine.

"It's nice here," I tell her. "The city's so -"

"No, I mean at the hotel," she says, interrupting me.

"I've never stayed here before," I reply.

She stares at me for a moment. Something about this whole conversation feels very stiff and awkward, as if we're both struggling to keep it going.

"You didn't tell me your name," she points out finally.

"Sorry. I'm Katie."

"Is that short for Catherine?"

I nod.

"And what's your surname, Catherine?"

"Johnson."

"I see."

I wait, but she seems strangely fixated on these little details, as if they really matter to her.

A moment later, hearing voices in the distance, I realize that Jason is coming back from the manager's office. I have to admit, that's a huge relief; it's almost as if he's saving me from this strange conversation.

"I shouldn't disturb you," Michelle says, taking a step back but keeping her eyes fixed on me. "Have a nice day out there. Maybe I'll see you tonight."

"Sure," I reply as she turns and walks away. "Thank you."

"Are you okay?" Jason asks, coming over to me. He turns and watches as Michelle disappears up the main staircase. "What did that woman want?"

"Nothing," I reply. "She's just a little odd, that's all. What was up with the manager?"

"Oh, it was just some nonsense about a promotion they're running," he replies, taking my hand and leading me toward the main door. "You know what they're like. They want you to sign up for another stay before you've even left. I told him we'd love to come back, but that we're not in a position to book anything right now."

"Sounds pushy," I mutter. "Do you want to know something weird? I swear I've met that Michelle woman somewhere before, but I just can't place where."

"She didn't look familiar to me," he replies as we step out into the sunshine. "Now come on, let's focus on having a great day."

EIGHTEEN

“AND THIS,” the tour guide says as we follow her into yet another of the castle's gloomy rooms, “is said to be where Baron Carfolle tortured his most important guests.”

“Nice,” I whisper under my breath as I look around and see thick metal rings attached to the walls.

“Now,” the guide continues, “remember what I said earlier. In the eighteenth century, a man like Baron Carfolle could effectively get away with whatever he wanted. There was no real oversight. People in the city could hear the screams of his victims, but what could they do about it? Nobody wanted to actually cross Carfolle, so they just had to let him get on with it.”

“Can I ask a question?” a woman says.

"Who were his victims, usually? Did he just kidnap people from the local area? Like, peasants and people like that?"

"He tortured anyone he could get his hands on," the guide explains, as we fan out across the room and look at the various chains and grim-looking devices. "Men, women, even children. No-one was safe. It's even said that he once had a group of nuns kidnapped and brought here, and that their screams and anguished prayers could be heard every night for a month."

"I guess a guy has to keep himself entertained somehow," Jason whispers to me with a smile.

"The gutters beneath your feet were designed to let the blood drain away," the guide continues. "Baron Carfolle actually employed people to go through the remains of his victims and remove anything that might possibly be valuable. In fact, the whole castle was designed to make it easier for the bodies to be removed. That's why, even today, Baron Carfolle is generally regarded as one of the most depraved torturers in all of European history."

I reach out and touch one of the metal rings.

"Other visitors to the castle were few and far between," the guide says. "As you can probably imagine, nobody really wanted to be a guest of a -"

Suddenly I hear an agonized scream,

accompanied by a sickly splitting sound, as if bones are slowly being broken. I keep my hand on the ring, overcome by a powerful stench of death, and a moment later there's the sound of some kind of saw starting up and beginning to grind through something dense. Closing my eyes, I try to force these horrible sounds from my head. I hear the scream continue, however, and now it's joined by a kind of guttural choking sound. The grinding noise continues, and now I'm certain that I can hear something cutting through bone. At the same time, someone in the distance is laughing.

I squeeze my eyes shut tighter.

"Honey?"

I let out a startled cry as I open my eyes and spin around, and I find that Jason is right behind me.

Everyone else has stopped to stare at me, and even the guide has fallen silent.

"Are you okay?" Jason asks with a faint smile on his lips. "Katie?"

"I'm fine," I say, feeling distinctly uneasy as everyone continues to stare at me. "Just... getting drawn into the history of the place, I guess."

"That's understandable," the guide replies, before turning to the others. She's a real pro. "In fact, a lot of people have reported a sense of dread here in this part of the castle. Now, I'm not one for ghost stories or anything like that, but even I have to admit that I sometimes feel a little unsettled if I'm here alone. And some of the other staff... Well, they refuse to work here at night. Some of them have reported hearing faint groans, and even seeing figures moving in the darkness."

As she continues to talk, I take a deep breath and try to pull myself together. There's a kind of cold, prickly sweat on my forehead, and I can't shake the feeling that I'm missing something. Or that I've *forgotten* something.

"Should I be worried?" Jason asks.

I shake my head.

"Maybe we should skip the second half of the tour," he continues, placing a hand on my shoulder. "It's a lot to take in. How about we go take a look at the gardens instead?"

I open my mouth to tell him that, no, I want to stay on the tour. Suddenly, however, I realize that I desperately want to get outside and breathe some fresh air. I never thought of myself as a particularly sensitive soul, but right now I can't handle the thought of hearing more about this disgusting Baron Carfolle guy.

"Come on," Jason says, taking my hand and leading me back across the room, as the guide continues to tell stories about the castle's past. "This was probably a bad idea. Who wants to hear all about some long-dead sadist, anyway?

NINETEEN

"I DON'T KNOW," I say to Jason as we sit on a bench in the castle's garden area, "I just feel... off."

"The way you felt before we came away?"

"No, it's different. It started after we arrived."

"Well, that's not supposed to happen," he replies. "Not on a relaxing vacation." He pauses. "Are you still thinking about the attack?"

"No," I reply, suddenly feeling self-conscious again about my scar. "Yes. Maybe. I don't know."

"You've been downplaying what happened," he continues, "but it must have been traumatizing. And then for that girl to try mugging you once we got here... That's two nasty incidents in the space of six months, Katie. It's no surprise that you're feeling a little troubled."

"I should be fine," I say as I look up at the castle's high walls. "I *want* to be fine. I want to be resilient."

"You *are* resilient," he tells me, placing a hand on my knee, "but no-one's completely immune to these things, honey. You're not a robot. Maybe it was a mistake to come here, maybe it was too much stress. We could have just had a relaxing weekend at home. Just the two of us."

"No, I love that we came away," I reply. "Damn it, this is all coming out totally wrong. I just -"

I blink, and in an instant I suddenly have a very strong image in my head. I see Michelle, the woman from the hotel, standing completely naked and covered in blood. She's grinning at me, but my attention is drawn to little white chunks that are trapped in the blood as it runs down over her large, teardrop-shaped breasts. As some of the chunks glint in the low light, I realize that they're fragments of bone. And Michelle's laughing, as if she's really enjoying herself.

"Katie?"

I turn to Jason, and now the image is fading.

"You look kinda pale there," he says, touching my forehead. "Are you sure you're not coming down with something?"

For a moment, I can't answer. All I can do is

think about the image of Michelle, and about the smile on her face. There was so much blood on her, it was flowing down her body, carrying the little bone chunks over all her contours and curves. And then, as I stare into space, I realize that Michelle is holding something in her right hand, some kind of grinder with large, serrated teeth. Behind her, meanwhile, there's a bloodied body strapped to a chair, shaking violently in slow motion as blood sprays from its torn throat.

It's as if Michelle has been torturing someone.

"Katie?"

I blink and see Jason again.

"Okay," he says, "I really think we should head back to the hotel and relax." He hesitates. "I know I keep asking you about this, and I'm sorry, but... You *are* taking your pills, aren't you?"

"What?" I feel momentarily confused, as if I don't know what he's talking about. "Yes. I mean, of course. I wouldn't dream of not doing that. You really *can* trust me, you know."

The truth, however, is that I haven't felt the same since I skipped that pill last night. I can't believe I was so stupid, missing a pill just so that I could be better in bed with Jason. I guess I just have to make sure that I never do anything like that again, and I have to wait for my mind and my body to get back to normal. I knew there'd be some small side effects from what I did last night, but I never expected crazy dreams and actual hallucinations. Maybe I just underestimated how much I need that medication.

"Let's take a nice stroll back to the hotel," Jason says, as he gets to his feet. "In fact, I've got a great idea about what we can do with our afternoon."

TWENTY

"ISN'T THIS AMAZING?" he asks as he swims over to me in the hotel's indoor pool. "I'm so glad there aren't many guests here at the moment, it means we get this place all to ourselves."

"It's lovely," I reply, standing in the shallow end and trying to find some way to make myself relax. "I hadn't even realized that they *have* a pool here. Then again, I knew basically nothing about the place before we arrived. That's what happens when your husband wants to surprise you."

Reaching me, he puts his hands on my shoulders, and for a moment he simply stares into my eyes. I wait for him to say something, but as the seconds pass I start to realize that he seems really worried. I guess I can't really blame him. This vacation was supposed to help me sort my head out, but instead I've arguably managed to get even worse. It's as if I'm teetering on the edge of some kind of breakdown.

"What?" I ask finally, feeling a little uncomfortable. "Jason, I'm sorry if I've been -"

"You don't have anything to be sorry about," he tells me. "I just hope you know you can be completely honest with me. About everything. If there's something on your mind, something that's worrying you, I want you to know that you can tell me. No matter how strange it might seem, no matter how worried you might be, you can tell me *anything*. I want to help you, if something feels wrong."

"Of course," I reply. "I *do* know that."

"Before it's too late," he adds.

I wait for him to continue, but now he's just staring at me again.

"Too late?" I ask. "Why... I mean, what do you mean?"

"If there's anything on your mind," he replies, "now would be a good time to tell me. That's all."

"There's nothing on my mind," I say cautiously, even though I'm not being entirely honest. "I mean, obviously there's stuff on my mind, but it's nothing worth sharing."

How *could* I share it? How could I tell him about that weird hallucination earlier, when I imagined Michelle covered in blood? How could I tell him about the screams I thought I heard while we were in the castle? How could I go into detail about my insane dream from last night? At the same time, I need to get all those things out of my head, because so far I'm doing a really bad job of hiding them.

Before I can say anything, however, I hear a door banging in the distance. Jason and I both turn just in time to see that Michelle and her husband are coming through to use the pool.

As she walks over to one of the loungers, Michelle glances at me and smiles.

"Great," Jason says quietly, "I guess the peace and solitude couldn't last forever, could it?"

"I'm fine," I reply, turning to him. "Honestly. In fact, I don't think I've ever been better. And that's really down to you, because you're the one who's kept me sane and strong through all of this. I haven't thanked you enough, but I should have done. You pretty much saved my life, Jason. I honestly don't think I'd be here without you."

"Of course you would," he says, "but I'm definitely glad that you let me come along with you for the ride."

Behind me, there's a rippling sound as someone slides into the water at the other end of the pool.

"When we get home," I continue, "I'm going

to be a better person."

"Katie," he says with a smile, "you don't need to -"

"I'm going to be a better wife," I add, "and a better... everything."

"You realize you're already perfect, don't you?"

"I'm going to be a better -"

Stopping suddenly, I feel as if there's a block in my mind, as if my thoughts have suddenly been prevented from going down a certain avenue. I try to push past, I try to force myself to remember, but the block is too strong and too powerful.

Behind me, someone is slowly swimming toward us.

"I'm going to..."

My voice trails off as I realize that I'm not sure how to complete that sentence.

"Jason," I say cautiously, "I know this is going to sound strange and maybe a little bit scary, but... I can't remember what I do for a living."

He tilts his head slightly, studying my face.

"What's my job?" I ask, trying very hard to not panic. "Jason, where do we live? I can't remember what our house looks like, or where it is. And what do *you* do?"

I pause.

Someone is swimming closer and closer.

"We don't have children, do we?" I

continue, as I realize that I can barely remember anything from before we arrived at the hotel. “No, we don't. I'd remember that, wouldn't I? I mean, nobody could forget something like that.”

I take a deep breath, but my head still feels wrong.

“And we don't have pets,” I add. “Or do we? Do we have a dog?”

Reaching up, I touch the scar on my face.

“How did I get this?” I ask.

“Katie,” Jason replies, “you're stressing about things. There's really no need.”

“I don't know who I am,” I tell him, as I feel the panic getting stronger and larger in my chest, spreading out to fill my entire body. “Jason, I don't remember anything!”

“I think you need to calm down,” he says firmly.

“How did I get the scar?”

He sighs.

Behind me, someone is still swimming. They sound so close now, they must be about to bump into me.

“I don't remember anything,” I stammer. “The first thing I remember, the very first thing, is... getting out of the taxi when we arrived here at the hotel. You asked me how I sleep, you made some crack about me being pretty, but I don't remember a single thing from before that moment. I don't remember being on a plane, and I don't remember being at home. Jason, I -"

Water splashes against the back of my neck.

I turn around, but there's nobody there.

And then, after a moment, Michelle pushes up and breaks the surface just a few feet away, and I watch as she slicks her hair back and grins at me. There's water all over her body, with little droplets dancing in the light.

"Oh, hey," she says, "sorry, I didn't mean to come so close. I thought I was going over to the other corner. I forgot my goggles."

Staring at her, as reflected light ripples in blue and white patterns against her skin, I can't help but think back to the image of her covered in blood.

"That's okay," Jason says stiffly after a moment, "my wife and I were just having a conversation."

"Then I can only apologize if I interrupted," Michelle replies.

"That's fine," Jason says, "but we'd like to continue now, if you don't mind."

"Of course. I'm so terribly sorry."

Michelle stares at me for a moment, before turning and starting to swim slowly and serenely away. I watch her for a few seconds, and then I turn to Jason again.

"You've been through a lot," he says, "and it's natural that you find things a little difficult.

Now, we could go over everything in great detail, or we could just relax for the rest of our vacation. I mean, you *do* actually remember your life, don't you?"

"I..."

I hesitate, and in that moment I realize that I remember some of it. Not everything, but enough to set me at ease. I'm a little hazy on the details, but at least I have a sense of who I am again. I remember my parents, and I remember some things from my childhood.

Suddenly Jason looks past me, and I turn to see that Henri from reception is standing at the other end of the pool, watching us.

"I have to go and have a quick word with someone about something," Jason tells me. "How about we both get dry, and I'll meet you out in the lobby?"

I turn to him.

"What's wrong?" I ask.

"Nothing. Probably just another sales thing, but I want to keep on their good side." He gives me a kiss on the cheek, but I can tell that he's worried. "Dry off, honey. I want our last night here to be perfect."

TWENTY-ONE

A QUICK WORD WITH someone about something.

As I sit in the changing room and replay Jason's words over and over in my mind, I can't help thinking that he's hiding something from me. I very nearly challenged him there and then, I very nearly insisted on going with him to speak to this manager, but at the last second I backed down. Now I really wish that I hadn't, because I'm sitting here with so many thoughts and worries rushing through my head.

Something's not right.

Hearing bare footsteps slapping against the wet floor, I turn just in time to see that Michelle has come through from the pool.

"Hey," she says with a smile as she heads to her locker, "I hope we didn't disturb you two lovebirds earlier. If we'd known you were in there, we wouldn't have come in. We could have done our swimming later."

"It's fine," I reply. "The pool's for everyone, right?"

"We only wanted a dip," she says, and suddenly she starts slipping out of her costume.

Before I really know how to react, she's standing completely naked in front of me. This woman certainly doesn't seem to be very shy.

"Is this your last day here?" she asks.

"Uh, yes," I say, trying very hard to keep from looking at her body. She's only a few feet away from me, so it's kind of difficult to not stare.

"Us too," she replies. "It's just a short weekend trip, really. A chance to relax and recharge our batteries. You have no idea how much I need this break right now."

She turns and bends down, reaching into her bag. I can't help looking at her breasts and noticing that they're exactly the same as I imagined them in my hallucination.

"Have you been to a Hotel Necro location before?" she asks.

"No," I reply. "I didn't know it was a chain."

"Oh, they have a few," she says airily, as if she's just chatting completely casually. "This is the first time we've been to this one, but we've tried quite a few of their other locations over the years. I know that might sound boring, but Dan and I are of the opinion that once you find something you really like, it doesn't make sense to keep searching for a place that's even better. And I have to admit, there's nowhere else quite like Hotel Necro. There's something so luxurious and exclusive about their brand."

"It seems really nice," I reply, as I start getting ready to leave.

Michelle takes a newspaper from her bag and sets it on the bench, and I can't help noticing the headline:

TECH CEO NOT MISSING INSISTS COMPANY AFTER MONTH-LONG SILENCE.

It's funny, but I don't think I've checked the news once since we got here. That's pretty unusual for me, I think. Or is it? I feel like the sort of person who'd like to know what's going on in the world, but – again – I can't really be sure. Everything from before we arrived here just seems kind of... hazy.

"It's so good to get away from everything, isn't it?" Michelle says after a moment, as she starts drying herself with a towel. "You know, I honestly think that a weekend here is enough to help me deal with the world for the next six months. And then I guess Dan and I will book ourselves right back in for another session." She smiles again. "That's the problem, really. You start to rely on these little luxuries. Did you know, if you book your next stay within a month of checking out, they give you a discount?"

"That sounds good," I reply, before getting to my feet. "I hope you enjoy the rest of your stay. I have to go and meet my husband now."

I turn and head toward the door.

"See you tonight," Michelle says.

I stop and glance back at her.

"Maybe, I mean," she adds. "Maybe see you tonight. If we're lucky."

TWENTY-TWO

ONE HOUR LATER, SITTING all alone in the lobby, I check my watch again and I realize that Jason doesn't seem to be coming. I've tried calling him, but his phone is off. I'm sure he said to meet here, but I guess it's possible that I misheard and he wanted to meet in the room instead. And to be honest, I'm getting a little sick of sitting around and waiting.

Sighing, I get to my feet and head toward the stairs.

TWENTY-THREE

"JASON?" I CALL OUT as I step into the room and set my bag down. "Honey, are you here?"

I let the door swing shut, but I can already tell that I'm alone. I head over and look at the bed, and then I take a look in the bathroom, but there's still no sign of him. I try calling again, but his phone remains off, and finally I stop and try to figure out what's happening.

Deep down, I can feel a flicker of worry in my gut, but I tell myself that he's just been delayed. Or, knowing Jason, he's headed out to concoct some grand romantic gesture for our final night here. So, instead of allowing myself to keep worrying, I grab my book and head over to the bed. Maybe, after everything that's been happening lately, it'd be good to have a few hours on my own.

I might even finally get my head straight.

TWENTY-FOUR

"NO, THAT'S FINE," I say over the phone, as I stand at the bedroom window and look out at the city. Rain is falling now, and the streets are pretty empty. "I just wanted to check whether my husband had left a message for me, that's all."

"There are no messages, I'm afraid," Henri replies. "Is there anything else I can help you with, M'am?"

"No, that was all," I tell him. "Thank you."

Cutting the call, I set the phone down and then I turn and look back out across the city. The weather out there is getting worse by the minute, and I keep hoping that I might spot Jason hurrying this way through the rain. His jacket is hanging in the wardrobe, but I guess maybe he simply wasn't expecting to be out for this long. I know that Jason's more than capable of taking care of himself, and I know I shouldn't worry, but I still can't rid myself of a nagging suspicion that maybe something really *is* wrong.

Suddenly remembering the safe in the wardrobe, I head over and type in the combination. When I look inside, I see that Jason's wallet is still in there. He put it there before we went down to the pool, and he'd certainly need to take it with him if he left the hotel. So I guess he's not out shopping.

"Where are you?" I whisper, still trying to suppress my sense of concern.

I stare into the safe for a moment longer, before turning and heading to the bathroom. As I walk, I make a decision. It's a little after 5pm right now. If Jason isn't back in one hour, I'm going to have to start thinking seriously about calling the police

TWENTY-FIVE

"ANSWER THE PHONE, DAMN you," I mutter as I pace back and forth across the room. "Come on, you're really starting to scare me."

Once again, however, the call is diverted straight to Jason's voicemail, and this time I figure that there's no point leaving yet another anxious message. I cut the call, and then I turn and look at the window as rain falls more heavily than ever. A moment after that, I glance at the clock next to the bed, and my heart sinks as I see that it's now almost 7pm. I'm well past the deadline I set for myself earlier, and I think it's finally time to accept that something's wrong.

My husband is missing.

I hesitate for a moment longer, and then – filled with a growing sense of panic – I grab my bag and hurry across the room. I pull the door open and start to step out into the corridor, only to slam straight into Jason.

"Where have you been?" I gasp, stunned but also hugely relieved to see him.

I wait, but he simply stares at me.

He looks upset, with a hint of tears in his eyes.

"Where have you been?" I ask again, but my relief is starting to turn to fresh dread. "Jason, talk to me. What happened?"

"Nothing," he murmurs, before stepping into the room and carefully shutting the door.

"You've been gone for hours!" I point out. "I tried calling you!"

"My phone must be out of battery."

"Where were you? Were you in the hotel? Did you go out somewhere?"

"I've been around," he replies, but he still seems strangely drained, almost blank. "I had something to do."

He makes his way past me, heading to the desk in the corner of the room.

"I was terrified!" I say finally, no longer worried about whether or not I sound crazy. "I was imagining all these awful things that might have happened to you! I was about to call the police!"

I wait, but he's busy connecting his phone to a charger. It's almost as if he didn't even hear me.

"I want to know what you've been doing for the past few hours," I continue. "Jason, I want to know where you went."

He mumbles something, but I can't quite make out the words.

"Jason," I say, stepping up behind him, "what -"

Suddenly he grabs the vase from the desk and throw it across the room, sending it smashing into the wall. I stare, shocked by his outburst, but then I remember that this – or something very similar – happened in my dream last night. I heard Jason destroying something in a fit of anger, and now as he turns to me I realize that he's struggling to contain his fury. For a few seconds, he seems to be almost boiling over with rage, and then finally he sighs and puts his hands over his face.

"Jason," I stammer, "I..."

I hesitate for a moment, before taking a step back. All day, I've been telling myself that the dream was *just* a dream, but Jason's outburst is making me think again. I want to ask him what's really happening, but finally I turn and hurry into the bathroom. Heading to my toiletry bag, I pull it open and start rooting around inside, but sure enough the little red pill is gone now. It must have been removed at some point after we went out this morning.

My mind is racing.

I pause, before pulling my pants down and taking another look at the puncture marks on my left leg. They're real, they're right there, they're...

Proof?

But if the marks are real, then that means that the dream...

"Looking for something?" Jason asks.

I turn and see him watching me from the doorway. He looks so anxious, and so disappointed. He looks like a man who's in serious trouble.

"Why did you do it, Katie?" he continues, as I pull my pants back up. "Everything was arranged, it was supposed to be easy. You just had to take your pills, and the whole trip would have been fine."

I open my mouth to ask what he means, but I can't quite manage to get the words out. There's something about the expression on Jason's face that's really scaring me.

"You remember, don't you?" he says. "They said you wouldn't, but then they didn't know at the time that you'd skipped one of your pills. Then they called me into the office this morning and showed me the camera footage, they showed me the moment last night when you hid one of the pills."

"Camera footage?" I reply, as my mind races to understand what's actually happening. "In the bathroom?"

"Camera footage in the bathroom," he says.

"Do you seriously think this place doesn't have camera coverage everywhere? They need to know everything that's going on."

"This is a bathroom!"

"They don't care."

"Jason..."

"I *knew* you were conscious last night," he continues. "Strickland swore that it was impossible, but I could see it in your eyes. Then this morning, when you talked about having a bad dream, I began to think that maybe you really believed that." He sighs. "I thought there was still a chance to salvage this thing and to make sure that the third night went ahead properly. But when they showed me the footage of you hiding the pill, I realized I was being a fool. So, in answer to your question about where I've been for the past few hours, I'll tell you. I've been begging them to reconsider their decision. I've been trying to persuade them not to kill you."

"What?" I reply, as I feel a cold shiver pass through my chest.

"They won't allow anything to happen that might jeopardize Hotel Necro."

"They want to kill me?" I ask, still convinced that this must be some kind of bad joke. "Why? What is this place? What happened to me last night?"

"Katie -"

"Forget it," I stammer, hurrying over and

trying to squeeze past him. "I have to -"

"No!"

Grabbing me by the shoulders, he shoves me back and presses me hard against the wall.

"If you try to run," he says firmly, as I continue to struggle, "you'll be dead before you get to the lobby. I'm not lying to you, Katie. I managed to persuade them that I can fix this, that I can get you to the end."

"The end?" I reply. "The end of what?"

"You just have to wait it out until the morning," he continues. "We're due to check out at 10am and go to the airport to fly home, and then everything'll be fine. You have to trust me on this, Katie. And the best part of the whole thing is, you don't really have to do anything. Just spend the evening with me as normal, take your pills, and then you'll wake up in the morning and you won't remember anything that happens tonight."

"What *will* happen tonight?" I ask. "What is this place, Jason?"

"There's no -"

"What is Hotel Necro?" I scream, struggling again to get free. "What aren't you telling me?"

"Katie -"

"What have you dragged me into?" I shout.

"I didn't drag you into anything!" he snaps. "You wanted to come here! You *chose* to come here! It was your idea! It's all your fault!"

"What?"

Sighing, he stares at me for a moment before taking a step back.

I want to run, but for a few seconds I hesitate.

"I'll prove it to you," Jason says finally, as he takes his phone from his pocket. "I'll show you the full truth. I'll show you that you're the reason for all of this."

TWENTY-SIX

"AND HOW EXCITED ARE you," Jason's voice asks in the video that's playing on his phone, "on a scale of one to ten?"

"I don't know," I reply on the screen, smiling slightly. "Nine? Ten?"

I watch myself laugh, and I feel a cold shiver in my chest. There's no doubt that this video shows me, but I don't remember any part of this conversation actually happening. On the screen, I have my hair tied back and I look to be wearing some kind of smart black dress, and I'm wearing more make-up than I'd ever normally wear. The scar is on my face, and it looks a little fresher. There's something else, too; my expression is different to anything I remember seeing on my face before. A little colder, maybe. A little calmer.

But it *is* me.

"So this time next week we'll be at Hotel Necro in Italy," Jason's voice continues, "and we'll be right in the middle of the whole experience. You know what that means, right?"

"Stop it," I reply on the video. "You're turning me on."

"Wait until we actually get there," he replies.

"I'm looking forward to it," Video Me tells him. "Now, do you mind if I get back to work? I can't just sit around here all afternoon like this. Some of us actually have serious responsibilities."

"Just one more question," Video Jason replies. "Do you think you'll have any problems with the... dirtier parts of the experience?"

Video Me hesitates, as if the question troubles her slightly.

"No," she says finally. "I think I'll be fine. I *know* I'll be fine. I mean, that's what this whole Hotel Necro thing is about, isn't it? It wouldn't work without the dirtier parts, as you so delicately describe them." Video Me still seems a little uncertain, but finally she forces a big smile. "I can't wait. I need this trip. I need it so much, I'm damn near ready to burst."

The video ends, and I'm left sitting on the edge of the bath, next to Jason. The words from the video are ringing in my head, but they still don't quite make sense. I can't deny that I'm the woman in that video, but why don't I remember any of that? Why don't I really remember very much at all?

"There's one more that you need to see," he says, bringing up a second video. "Hotel Necro requires all guests to record one of these, in case of emergencies. I think this counts as an emergency."

He plays the video, and I see myself on the screen once again.

"My name is Katie Johnson," I'm saying with a faint smile, "and I'm twenty-nine years old, and of sound mind. Well, some people might question that, but anyway... I'm recording this video because I want to make it clear that I'm doing the whole Hotel Necro thing willingly. I *want* to do it. And if something goes wrong, I want to state on the record that I'm going into this with my eyes open. I know what happens at Hotel Necro, and I want to do it. I'm a little nervous, but that's all. I'm totally up for this." The video version of me turns and looks past the camera. "Is that okay? Is that enough?"

"Do you have a message for yourself," Video Jason asks, "if for whatever reason you're watching this and you don't quite understand?"

Video Me hesitates, before looking into the camera again.

"Just be cool," she says. "Don't over-think things, don't stress, and don't screw it up. Trust Jason. You know he'd never do anything bad, right?

Just accept that you don't understand everything, and push on through. You'll be so glad that you did. You need this experience. For your sanity. Now go and enjoy it." She smiles. "Peace out!"

The video ends.

I have a million questions, but I can't get any of them out. I simply sit in silence, trying to work out exactly what's happening to me.

"People like you come to a place like this because they need to let off steam," Jason explains after a moment. "You spend all your time running your company, Katie, and your stress levels are off the scale. You also have enough money and connections to try an unorthodox approach to that problem. Hotel Necro allows you to... unleash an aspect of yourself that you'd usually keep hidden. We all have that aspect, but we keep it contained. Doctor Strickland's program at Hotel Necro is based on the belief that any individual will gain untold benefits from a short, focused period of unrestrained violence. It's kind of like getting back to your inner caveman."

I wait for him to continue. This has to be some kind of joke.

"You can do anything at Hotel Necro," he adds. "*Anything*, Katie. And because your memory of it all is suppressed, you get all the subconscious benefits without any of the guilt. All your stress will be gone, and the effect will last for at least six months, maybe even longer."

I start slowly shaking my head.

"You took a few pills before we came here," he explains, "just to get you started. That's why you might not remember much of your actual life. It's actually perfectly normal."

"I run a tech company," I reply, struggling to think back to the time before we came to this place. "It's small, it's a start-up."

"That's right. The pills you take in the morning here are the ones that increase production of certain hormones. Those hormones allow you to overcome your inhibitions during the nights, which is when we go down to the main rooms beneath the hotel. The round pill, which is the one you skipped last night, makes sure that you don't remember anything in the morning."

"Jason," I say cautiously, "none of this makes any sense. It's like something out of some dumb movie."

"The important thing is that you won't remember any of this," he says firmly. "All you have to do, Katie, is get through the next twenty-four hours. Less than that, even. Fourteen, fifteen hours at most. Do exactly what I tell you to do, and we both get to walk out of here, but if you try to break the rules in any way..."

His voice trails off for a moment.

"What you say next is very important," he

adds. “Remember that they can hear us.”

“Who can?”

“The whole building is bugged from top to bottom.”

I take a deep breath.

Looking around, all I see is a normal hotel bathroom. There's no sign of any cameras or microphones, but I guess those things can be pretty tiny. Is it true? Are we really being watched right now?

“You have to stay strong,” Jason says firmly. “Trust me, Katie. Once you're away from here, you'll be glad that you listened to me. Once you get home, you'll feel all the benefits of this trip and none of the guilt. *None* of it. It'll all make sense, I promise, but you *have* to trust me. You heard what you said in the video.”

He reaches over to take my hand, but I pull away.

“Katie -”

“Go to Hell,” I reply, getting to my feet and hurrying out of the bathroom.

“Katie!” he calls out as I race to the door and pull it open. “Don't be stupid, you're making a terrible mistake! You're in over your head!”

I start heading along the corridor, but I stop after just a couple of paces as I see two men waiting ahead. They're wearing dark suits and dark glasses, and I immediately realize that they mean business. I stare at them for a moment, before turning just as Jason comes out of the room behind me.

"Everything I told you is true," he says with a hint of fear in his voice. "If you try to fight it, they'll kill you. If you try to call the police, they'll kill you. The police know better than to come here, anyway. But if you just stick to the original plan, to the plan that you agreed to before we came here, then everything will be fine. And when we get home, and your head is clear again, you won't remember what happened here but you *will* fell all the benefits of the process. You heard what you said on the video, Katie. You trust yourself, don't you?"

Staring at him, I realize that he's serious.

"You have to decide, Katie," he continues. "If you've ever trusted *me*, I'm begging you... Trust me now. And trust the version of you from that video."

TWENTY-SEVEN

SITTING ON THE END of the bed, I listen to the sound of Jason brushing his teeth.

I can't do this. I keep telling myself that I have to get out of here, but at the same time I know that I have no choice. The woman in that video *was* me, and there's no way a deep fake could be that convincing. I still don't cntircly understand what's going on here at Hotel Necro, but I feel as if I'm caught up in something that's way bigger than me. I keep telling myself that those guys in the corridor wouldn't *actually* have hurt me. At the same time, I didn't dare to take the risk.

For a moment, I imagine what would have happened if I'd tried to run. In my mind's eye, I see a scene from some bad action movie, as the two men aim guns at me and fire. I see myself falling to the ground, and I see Jason racing over to me. But...

That wouldn't actually have happened, would it?

I swallow hard.

Maybe I'm a bad person, but I figure I just have to take the easy way out now. I have to take the pills, and then tomorrow morning I'll wake up and I won't remember what happens during the night.

Easy.

End of story.

I just have to take the easy way out for once.

The tap turns off, and a moment later Jason emerges from the bathroom with a glass of water in one hand and two red pills – one round and one oblong – in the other.

"Please don't take this the wrong way," he says, stopping in front of me, "but I'd kinda like to *see* you swallow them. The guys watching on the cameras will too."

"Were they watching when we..."

My voice trails off as I think back to the two times we made love in this room. Then I think about all the times I was in the bathroom, all the times I took a pee or went in the shower. Even the times I pooped. Was I being watched while I was doing those things? The thought sends a shiver through my body.

"You accepted all of that before we came,"

he replies. “Remember what you said on the video. Once we get home, you'll understand.”

I look at the pills, and for a moment I consider not taking them. Then again, maybe those guys from the corridor would come back. Maybe they're waiting out there now, in case I decide to rebel.

“One more night,” Jason says softly. “You won't even remember it. You can do this.”

“Can't we just leave?” I ask. “If I promise to never say anything...”

“That's not how this works, Katie. You have to go through the full experience. It's one of their rules. Once you start, you can't stop until you're done.”

I hesitate, and then I reach out and take the pills from the palm of his hand. I look at them for a moment, before slipping them into my mouth and then taking the glass of water and washing the medication down. Except, at the last moment the oblong pill catches between my teeth and my cheek, and I let it stay there as I swallow the last of the water and hand the glass back to Jason.

“All done?” Jason asks. “Do I need to check?”

“All done,” I reply, shocked that by sheer luck one of the pills didn't go down. Or was it luck? I think I might have done it on purpose, albeit subconsciously. It's hard to be sure.

“You've made the right choice,” he says.

“I hope so.”

“You'll get tired soon.”

“I know.”

“Once we get home, you won't remember having been here. Not any of the details, at least. But you'll feel the benefits, Katic. It's gonna bc so good for you.”

“What about *you*?” I ask. “Will you remember?”

“Yeah,” he replies. “One person in a couple has to be less immersed than the other. I agreed to do this for you, because I love you. I mean, you practically begged me.” He stares at me for a moment. “It hasn't been easy.”

“What do I do when I get down there?” I ask. “Down to the rooms under the hotel, I mean.”

“You lose all your inhibitions.”

“But what exactly does that mean?”

“It means that you loosen up,” he explains. “That's all I'm allowed to tell you right now. I'm sorry, Katie.”

“Do you really think this is the right thing for me to do?” I ask.

He pauses, and then he nods.

“Then I guess I have to trust you,” I continue, “don't I?”

“You won't regret it,” he says, leaning down and kissing the top of my head. “Now why don't we get to sleep? They'll come for us around midnight."

As he makes his way to his side of the bed, I take a deep breath and try to keep from throwing up. I feel really nauseous, but I guess that's because I'm so totally nervous. Still, I tell myself that I can do this, and – as I head around the bed and climb in – I tell myself that I should just swallow the second pill. It's the oblong one that's still in my mouth, and I think Jason said that's the one that makes it so that I won't remember what happens tonight.

But I want to remember.

I want to know.

"Feeling tired?" he asks, leaning over and kissing me on the cheek.

I nod.

"And nervous?"

I nod again.

"This time tomorrow, we'll be home," he continues. "Everything'll be okay, and you'll get back to your normal life."

"Did I really understand everything that this involves?" I ask, turning to him. "Did I make a totally informed decision about coming here?"

"You did," he says firmly. "We even joked about what would happen if you somehow realized halfway through. Of course, you're not the first person this has happened to. Others have figured it out as well, but that's okay. They have a system in place to deal with that. You might even say that it's all part of the fun, and it certainly won't have a detrimental impact on the benefits you'll feel. Less than twelve hours to go, and then we'll be all done here."

He pauses, before putting a hand on my thigh.

"Do you want to loosen up a little first?" he asks, slipping his hand between my legs.

"Not tonight," I reply, reaching down and moving his hand away, as I glance at the walls and wonder where the cameras are hidden. "I just want to get this whole thing over with."

"I understand."

He kisses me again.

"Good night," I reply, rolling onto my side and staring at the wall.

I wait, and after a moment Jason switches off the light, plunging the room into darkness. For all I know, there might well be night vision cameras here in the bedroom, so I hesitate for a moment before carefully rolling over. As I do so, I manage to surreptitiously spit the oblong pull out of my mouth, and then – while pretending to fluff my pillow – I push the pill past the top of the bed and send it into the crack between the mattress and the wall.

I still don't quite understand what's going to happen tonight, but one thing's certain. At least now, I'll remember every moment once it's all over.

TWENTY-EIGHT

"MS. JOHNSON, WAKE UP."

Suddenly I open my eyes and find myself face to face, once again, with Doctor Strickland.

"How are you feeling?" he asks.

"I..."

For a moment, I'm a little confused. I feel as if I only shut my eyes in bed a few seconds ago, but now I'm standing in one of the rooms beneath the hotel. It's the same room where I found myself yesterday, although this time I quickly determine that I can move my body. A moment later I hear a bumping sound, and I turn to see the two orderlies pushing the trolley out into the corridor.

"That's better," Doctor Strickland says, stepping aside and gesturing for me to move forward. "I think perhaps -"

Before he can finish, an agonized scream rings out from somewhere in the distance. I flinch as I look toward one of the doors, and I listen as the scream dies down to a pained, pitiful gurgle.

"You'll be joining them shortly," Strickland continues as he takes a syringe from one of the tables and comes over to me. "Now, I just need to give you this hormone activator, and you'll be ready to go."

I don't react as he slides the needle into my arm, and I watch as he presses down on the plunger. A pale green liquid is sent into my body, and I take a deep breath as the needle slides back out.

"How do you feel?" Strickland asks.

"I feel... fine," I say cautiously.

"That's good. I understand that you took both the pills this time."

I nod.

"Then I hope you have a very enjoyable night," he says, as Jason comes through from one of the other rooms. "As ever, I'll be around if you have any questions."

"You're naked," I say to Jason, before looking down and realizing that I am too.

I blink.

I feel so... dazed.

I move my hand down, to cover myself, but then I hesitate. Does it really matter? I've always been very squeamish, maybe even prudish, but suddenly I feel an exhilarating buzz as I think of people seeing me like this. I guess those fresh hormones are rushing through my body, because I watch Strickland heading over to one of the other benches and I actually feel sad that he's not ogling me right now. I want him to look at my bare body, I want him to stare at every inch of me, I want him to start slobbering like a beast and -

"Katie?"

I turn to Jason, just as he takes my hand in his.

What's wrong with me? Why am I feeling so excited by all of this? Can a pill really change me that much?

"I've arranged a very special surprise for you tonight," Jason says, leading me toward a door that opens out into a long, dark corridor. "It wasn't easy, but I had a few leads and eventually, well, I guess we got a little lucky too. I think you're going to really appreciate this."

We pass an open doorway, and when I look through I see that Michelle is kneeling on the floor. She's naked, covered in blood, and she's holding a severed head. Next to her, a decapitated corpse is still bleeding onto the bare cobbles. My first thought is that this is all fake, that the body parts are dolls, but after a moment I realize that they seem very real.

"Good evening, there," Michelle says with a

smile, as she turns the head around so that I can see its dead face. "Do you know, I've always wanted to cut someone's head off. You should have heard the sounds he made while I was sawing through his throat." She visibly shudders with what I can only assume is some kind of extreme pleasure. "I actually slowed down so that I could enjoy it more. I was so sorry when he died."

Her husband Dan steps up behind her, and I watch as his large, erect penis brushes against the side of her face.

"I think I'm going to go and do it again," Michelle continues. "There's another one, a girl, they've procured for me. I'm going to do it even more slowly this time. I'm going to start by slicing off her nose. They always look so funny when they don't have a nose."

Getting to her feet, she turns and follows her husband through another doorway, carrying the head as she goes.

"That woman is definitely getting her money's worth out of this place," Jason says. "According to Strickland, she's surprising even the more seasoned staff at the hotel. Apparently she's very ingenious when it comes to her torture methods."

I want to tell him that this is sick and wrong, but somehow those words never leave my lips. Instead, I feel a kind of strange, blank emptiness, as if all my empathy has been washed away. Is there something wrong with me? I'm staring at a real, decapitated body, and I actually feel *good* about it all. There's a tiny part of me, tucked away deep in my mind, that's screaming at me and telling me that I have to run. Strangely, however, that scream just seems so utterly unimportant right now. It's just a beautiful, smooth thing, like the sculpture in the office.

"Come on," Jason says, leading me further along the corridor. "You're gonna love this."

We pass another door, and I look through just in time to see a man carrying a red hot poker toward a woman who's strapped over a table with her legs wide apart.

"Help me!" the woman screams as we walk past. "Please, you have to -"

She screams just as I lose sight of her, but I hear the sound of burning skin as I follow Jason toward the door at the far end of the corridor. I should be feeling disgusted, but instead there's a tightening knot of anticipation in my chest as I start to wonder what's waiting for me.

"This is going to be even better than Friday," Jason says.

"Friday?"

"The first night here," he continues, glancing back at me. "You were using a pair of scissors to slice off the front of a woman's eyeballs.

She actually got a hand free for a moment and grabbed you, you might have noticed a slight cut on your waist. In fact, I think I remember you mentioning a bruise and a cut on your side." He peers down at my bare waist. "Yeah, it's still there," he adds. "You definitely made her pay, though. You ended up hollowing out her eye sockets with a scalpel while she was still alive, and then you poured acid into the holes until they overflowed and it all ran down her face."

"*I* did that?" I reply, shocked but not as shocked as I would have expected.

"It's primal, honey," he says as we reach the door and he pushes it open. "It's something we've lost in modern society. It's the thrill of violence. Honestly, a few nights at Hotel Necro would do wonders for anyone's mental health. Of course, if it wasn't exclusive, maybe it wouldn't work quite so well. I guess this is one of the many benefits of being rich."

We step into a small room, and I immediately freeze as I see that there's a naked woman strapped to a chair at the far end. She has a thick white gag in her mouth, and she's shaking violently as she tries desperately to get free. Tears are streaming down her face, and she starts shaking even more as soon as she sees us.

"What are you feeling?" Jason asks.

"I should be horrified," I reply, as I feel the

knot of anticipation starting to tighten even harder in my chest, "but actually I feel... curious."

"That's the hormone release," he explains. "It's designed to strip away all the restraints that have built up in your mind. Now you're free to really let rip." He hesitates. "Well? You recognize her, don't you?"

"Recognize her?" Staring at the terrified girl, I realize that she *does* seem a little familiar.

"It's the bitch who tried to mug you yesterday," Jason says. "I pulled some strings and got the people here to go and snatch her off the streets." Leaning closer, he kisses me on the cheek. "For you. From me. A sign of my love. Think of her as an early birthday present. Now tell me, what are you going to do to her first?"

"First?" Staring at the girl, I suddenly feel a smile starting to spread slowly across my lips. "I think it's going to be really hard to decide."

TWENTY-NINE

SHE'S SCREAMING, OR AT least *trying* to scream. The gag muffles the sound, but she's struggling desperately as I start slowly closing a pair of metal shears against her left index finger. I watch as the blades start slicing through her skin, and then I feel the crunch of bone beneath.

This is all so... satisfying.

I hesitate, still wondering how all my empathy and compassion can be gone, and then I squeeze the handle tighter and watch as the top of her finger is sliced clean away.

Blood pours from the wound.

“So delicate,” Jason purrs, watching from nearby. “Don't you want to go crazy? Get a little frantic? I thought you'd want to really let rip.”

“I do,” I reply, as the girl strains every part

of her body in a desperate attempt to escape from the chair, "but I want to build up to it. How old do you think she is, anyway?"

"She's twenty-two," he tells me. "Pathetic, right? Begging and mugging people on the street like that. Call me crazy, but I have a feeling that society won't really miss her all that much. You could even argue that we're doing the world a favor."

"I suppose you could," I murmur, before setting the shears aside and looking at all the other devices on the bench.

"Maria Binotto," he continues, reading from a sheet of paper. "The fine people at Hotel Necro managed to pull together quite a trove of information about her. I guess that kind of thing's easy when you've got allies and sources in the police and government." He steps closer. "Twenty-two, like I said. Born and raised in a poor part of town, got a break when her grandmother died and left her enough money to get a proper education. She squandered all of that, however, and turned to drugs. Her parents threw her out, she ended up living on the streets and started racking up a series of petty criminal offenses. Some jail time here and there. Nothing about violent crimes, but I guess she must have finally become too desperate." He looks over at the girl. "Is that right, Maria? Did you fall in with an even worse crowd?"

As I stare at the assorted saws, clamps, knives and other torture devices, I feel a curious lack of empathy for the girl. Even the other day, when she mugged me, I felt a sliver of compassion, but that's all gone now. No doubt this is caused by the various pills in my system, but it's still odd to be so aware of this hollowness in my heart. And yet, at the same time, I'm still *me.* It's just that my empathetic, caring side has been suppressed to the point that it's now just the tiniest, faintest scream in the back of my mind.

"She's been whoring herself about, too," Jason says as he comes over and sets the sheet of paper down. "She's not worth giving a damn about, Katie. The world will definitely be better off without her. What are you going to do to her next?"

"Are you insane?" I imagine myself screaming. "I'd never hurt anyone!"

"What's this for?" I ask instead, picking up a small silver device that's shaped a little like a harp that's missing part of its center.

"I was hoping you'd ask," Jason replies with a grin, taking the device and then carefully turning a wheel at one end, causing the middle part to start closing. "It's a nice little nipple clamp. It also doubles as the jaw part of a makeshift electrocution system. There are some wires over in that box, you can hook it up and slowly cook the girl. Although, that part's a little risky, so they recommend leaving it until closer to the end. You don't want to kill Maria too quickly and squander what could be hours of fun."

I set the clamp down and pick up a hammer instead. There are so many weird and wonderful devices on this table, it's somewhat refreshing to see something as simple as a hammer.

"Now you're thinking better," Jason continues, as Maria desperately struggles in the chair. She's still trying to scream. "Think about what she did to you in that street. Think about what she would have done, if I hadn't interrupted."

Again, I feel some part of my soul start to resist, only for that part to be somehow blocked. I turn the hammer around, admiring its form, and then I find my mind starting to wander. I think of all the things I can do to hurt the girl in the chair, and I'm surprised to find that my imagination is quite unfettered in this regard. Awful, horrible ideas flood into my thoughts until I realize that it's quite hard to just pick one of them.

"What are you thinking?" Jason asks. "Face? Ribs? Jawbone?"

"I'm thinking..."

My voice trails off for a moment.

"I'm thinking..."

"I'd go for her hands," he whispers. "It'll be like the old medieval punishment for a thief. Destroy her hands first, then maybe her feet."

I nod slowly, even though I'm actually thinking of doing something much more spectacular. Much more grandiose. I remember seeing a picture during our tour of the castle, and I'm inspired by something that Baron Carfolle apparently used to do to his victims. Back then, of course, I was absolutely horrified by the idea. But back then, I hadn't taken a little pill that removes all my guilt. And where there should be a part of me that's screaming for all of this madness to stop, instead I simply feel calm as I turn and look over at Maria.

She's staring at me and sobbing, and still trying to pull herself free from her restraints.

“Do it,” Jason says. “Whatever you're thinking about, just do it.”

I swallow hard, and then I make my way back over toward the girl. I can feel a sense of anticipation building in my chest, rising up through my body and promising untold pleasure. I adjust my grip on the hammer slightly and then I raise it high, and the poor girl starts struggling harder than ever. I stare into her eyes and take a deep breath, trying to absorb some of her terror and turn it into gold. Like some kind of pain alchemist, I savor the moment for a few seconds and then I focus on making sure that my aim is true. And then, finally, I allow myself to strike.

I bring the hammer crashing down against

her left knee, and she tries once again to scream as I feel her kneecap shatter. The most shocking part is... this feels so good.

I hit the knee again, then again, each time breaking more bone until finally I step back and see that her left leg is now bent unnaturally at that spot, almost doubling back on itself. The skin is broken in a few places, but there's clearly lots of blood pooling just beneath the surface.

After taking another deep breath, I set to work on her other knee, smashing it with force and relishing each cracking sound that I hear. It's as if I'm battering the whole leg into submission, as if I'm some kind of sculptor, and I only stop when I finally realize that this leg too is now bent in the wrong direction at the knee.

Still conscious, and clearly in agony, Maria is straining every part of her body in a desperate attempt to pull herself out of the chair. She has no chance, of course, but it's still strangely satisfying to watch her struggle.

"It's like being a child again, isn't it?" Jason says. "You've caught some insignificant little bug and you're torturing it. It's part of everyone's instinct, Katie."

"Not quite," I reply, staring mesmerized as Maria continues to fight back. "She's not insignificant. It wouldn't be so much fun that way."

"Fair point."

I watch for a moment longer, before setting the hammer aside.

"You're taking your time more tonight," Jason tells me. "On the first night, you jumped in with more enthusiasm, but tonight you seem a little colder, like you're actually enjoying it more. I like that side of you."

"Is this really all it takes?" I reply, still staring at Maria as she struggles. "Are a couple of little pills really enough to let anyone do what I'm doing right now?"

"Apparently so."

"That's so... surprising," I add, as I feel a faint shudder pass through my bones. "It's hard to believe that everyone's wandering around in the real world, acting totally normal, and yet they're two pills away from being able to do this to another living person."

"Is it *really* that surprising?" he replies. "We've both seen people snap in crowds. Seen little bursts of anger and hatred. Hell, I even worked in retail when I was a kid. I've never had a very positive view of human nature."

"Mmm," I murmur, as I try to decide what I want to do next to Maria.

"Why don't you do her eyes?" Jason asks. "You enjoyed doing that to the woman the other night."

"No, I want to see her eyes until the end," I

reply, and then I settle on my next move. “I've got a better idea.” I turn to him. “Spread her legs for me. I'm going to find a pair of scissors.

THIRTY

SOMEONE SCREAMS IN THE distance, and the cry seems almost to echo through all the rooms before fading into an agonized, gurgled groan.

"Taking a break, M'am?"

Turning, I see that a man in a uniform has come around to the other side of the bar. My first instinct is to turn away, to cover my nakedness, but then some other drive kicks in and I sit up straight, allowing him a full view of my breasts.

"Drink, M'am?" he continues.

"What have you got?" I ask.

"I'm afraid we only serve non-alcoholic beverages down here," he explains. "The management prefers people to remain fully sober for the experience. Plus, there have been some cases where alcohol has interfered with the medication."

"What kind of cases?"

"I'm not at liberty to discuss such matters. Would you perhaps like to try one of our fabulous virgin mojitos?"

"Sure," I reply, and I watch as he goes to start making my drink. "So do *you* have to take pills?" I ask after a moment. "To work here, I mean."

At that moment, as if to underline my point, another scream briefly rings out.

"I just stay here at the bar," he replies calmly, "and I don't venture into any of the other rooms. That arrangement suits me just fine."

"And you can handle the screams?"

He glances at me for a moment, before turning back to the various bottles.

Sitting silently for a moment, I feel as if I'm being torn in two directions. There's a part of me that's totally happy with this situation, that just wants to carry on torturing that poor girl. At the same time, there's a part of me that feels I *should* be horrified by everything that's happening. It's almost as if, by taking that little red pill, I was able to temporarily suspend a part of my soul, and that's a strange thought. Have I always been able to do these awful things, and all I needed was a pill?

Looking down, I see some of Maria's blood on my breast. I start smearing the blood across my nipple, and for a moment I'm mesmerized by the patterns in the swirl.

"One virgin mojito," the barman says as he sets a green drink in front of me. "If you don't mind the observation, M'am, you seem... troubled."

"I'm not," I reply quickly. "That's the thing. I guess I'm just wondering how that can be possible."

"You weren't this philosophical on Friday night."

"Did we meet on Friday night?"

He smiles and nods.

"And how did I seem then?"

"You were laughing with your husband," he replies. "You had a lot more blood on your body, and at one point you were kissing one of the other guests. A lady who is also here tonight."

"I don't remember any of that," I tell him.

"That's simply how things work here at Hotel Necro," he explains. "I can assure you, however, that on Friday night you and the other lady were sitting over in that corner, and you got to know one another extremely well. Your husbands joined in, too. Let's just say that everyone seemed to be in a very sharing mood. And then, after a while, you all went back into the other rooms and I heard more screams. Everyone seemed to very much enjoy the experience."

I try to remember any of that, but there seems to be yet another block in my mind.

"The best thing," he continues, "is to just throw yourself into it all. Don't analyze it too much. In a few hours' time, you'll wake up in your nice clean bed upstairs and you won't remember any of this. You'll be back to normal, except for the fresh sense of calm in your mind."

"And you really think that works, huh?"

"I've heard Doctor Strickland's views on the matter," he replies, "and he seems to be a very knowledgeable guy. Hotel Necro has been here for a long time, and as far as I know nobody has ever complained about their stay. If you ask me, we're providing a good service that helps make the world a better place. Anyway, what do I know? I'm just a bartender, it's not my place to -"

Suddenly another screams fills the air, cutting him off. As the scream continues, twisting into a howl of agony, the barman simply smiles at me as if he's waiting for an end to – at most – a minor interruption.

"We're providing a good service," he continues finally, as the scream dies down, "that helps make the world a better place. For ladies and gentlemen such as your good selves. Besides, most of the victims here are trash. And who care about trash, right?"

I can still hear someone whimpering in the distance, and after a moment I realize that the victim in question is actually talking.

“Just kill me,” a man's voice is sobbing. “I just want this to end!”

“Are you not convinced?” the barman asks.

I open my mouth to answer him, but at the last moment I realize that maybe I should be a little more careful. After all, this guy works for Hotel Necro, and I'm sure that our conversation is being monitored. Jason was adamant that we'd be in danger if the people here suspected me of having doubts, and I'm not sure that I'm willing to take any kind of risk just now. Besides, the honest truth is that any doubts or fears in my heart are just the ghosts of emotions I feel that I *should* have. Right now, I'm already starting to think about what I'll do to that Maria girl when I go back through to the room.

“Thanks,” I say to the barman as I get to my feet. “I have things to do now.”

“Aren't you going to touch your drink?”

I look at the mojito, but I feel sick to my stomach and I think maybe it'd be better to not drink or eat anything at the moment.

“I'm sure it's great,” I tell him, “but I think I just need to get back. My husband will be waiting.”

With that, I turn and walk away. I think I can still feel the 'real' me screaming somewhere deep down, but she's totally impotent. I'll most likely be utterly horrified by all of this in the morning, but right now I just want to get back to the room and see what other awful things I can do to Maria. The awful truth is that Jason was right; I *am* enjoying this, and I *do* want to continue. The pills have woken a part of me that I never thought existed. And, at least until this night is over, I'm going to let that part of my soul out to play.

THIRTY-ONE

"HEY! LOOK AT THIS!"

As I head toward the door at the far end of the corridor, I stop and turn to see Michelle standing in one of the other rooms. She's towering over a sobbing man who's bound and gagged on the floor, and the man is already covered in cuts and bruises.

"I finished with the head of thc othcr onc," Michelle says, pointing toward a bloodied skull on the far side of the room. "I scratched most of the flesh off. Next time, I'm going to do it while the bastard's still alive. I don't know why I didn't think of that sooner. That's the thing, every time I'm done with one of these people, I think of ways I could have made it feel even better."

Not really knowing what to say, I look at the shivering man on the floor.

"You know," Michelle continues, "they give us all these torture devices, and sometimes it's like being a kid in a candy shop. But at the end of the day, isn't it better to keep things simple? Primordial, even. That's why I think I'm going to go old school on this miserable piece of shit." She pauses, staring down at him with a ravenous look in her eyes. "I'm going to beat him to death with my bare hands."

"Okay," I murmur.

"Do you want to watch?" she asks, turning to me. "I can't let you join in, because I want it to be all me, but I don't mind you watching. In fact, I think I'd like it."

"I'm... okay, thanks," I reply cautiously.

"Got your own thing bubbling away, huh?" she says, as she crouches in front of the guy. "I understand that. I even respect it. There's something about this place that really invites a sense of solitude. Dan's off in another room, I don't even know what he's doing, but I like that we each have our own separate projects." She reaches out and gently touches the side of her victim's head, as he stares up at her with pure terror in his eyes. "It's a profound connection, isn't it, this one between us? Between the one who's about to die, and the one who's about to do the killing."

The man tries to say something, no doubt begging for his life, but Michelle merely stares at him and – after a few seconds – begins to smile.

And then, suddenly, she sets his head back down and punches him hard, breaking his nose. Blood starts flowing from his nostrils, and Michelle watches for a few seconds before punching him again, this time in the throat.

"I'll leave you to it," I say, turning and walking away. As I do so, I hear a series of heavy, hard punches, accompanied by the sound of breaking bones.

Passing another door, I hear a slow cracking sound, and I look through just in time to see that Michelle's husband Dan is turning a large wheel. The wheel is attached to a long table, and there's a woman strapped in place. I stop for a moment, and to my horror I realize that this is some kind of medieval-style rack. The woman's arms and legs are held in place, and Dan is slowly turning the wheel and stretching her. While there's no gag in the woman's mouth, she seem unable to let out more than a faint gurgle, and I realize after a moment that her arms look to have already become dislocated.

"Want to join in?" Dan asks, turning to me. "This thing has an electric compressor, makes it slightly easier to push. I switched it off, though. I wanted to do this myself. With my own muscles."

"No, I'm fine," I reply, watching as the wheel continues to turn.

Suddenly a rupture bursts through the woman's belly as she's literally torn apart. Blood bursts from the gap, gushing down onto the floor, yet Dan continues to turn the wheel until I see the woman's internal organs starting to slop out from within her belly. After a moment I'm able to see part of her skeleton, her pelvis perhaps, but I can't stop watching as she's slowly pulled apart at the middle. She lets out a final groan, and it's hard to believe that she's somehow still clinging to life, but finally the last strands of flesh are broken and she's left in two halves on the rack.

"Impressed?" Dan asks, turning to me and then holding his arms up, flexing his muscles. "That wasn't easy."

"I'm sure it wasn't," I tell him, before walking away and heading toward the door at the far end.

I can still hear Michelle kicking her victim to death in the distance, but I have no real desire to go back and watch. After all, why stare at someone else as they have their fun, when it's possible to get really down and dirty? And as I open the door and see Maria still strapped to the chair, I feel a strange sense of tingling anticipation in my chest. This is it. This is what the whole night has been building toward. This is my chance to kill the bitch.

As Jason turns to me and smiles, I gently shut the door.

THIRTY-TWO

"WE'VE GOT BLADES AND saws and clamps," Jason explains as I step past him and make my way toward Maria. "We've got acids and batteries and pumps, we've got cheese graters, we've got hammers and drills. If there's anything you want, and we don't have it, just let me know and I'm sure the fine people from Hotel Necro can rustle it up. The world's your oyster, Katie. What do you want to do to her next?"

I barely hear him.

All I care about is the girl in the chair.

I make my way across the room, while keeping my gaze fixed on her terrified stare. She starts shaking violently again, more violently with each step that I take toward her. I feel more powerful than I've ever felt before in my life, and as

I stop and stare down at her face I realize that there's nothing holding me back. I can slash and rip and burn, I can tear her to pieces, and I don't even have to care.

Reaching down, I run a finger's edge across her belly, up over her breasts and then onto her neck. As I move my finger to her jaw, she lets out an anguished, muffled whimper and turns her head away, as if she still thinks that she can somehow save herself.

As if she thinks I might suddenly change my mind.

The funny thing is, it's her hope that I enjoy the most. If she just accepted her fate and begged to die, I wouldn't be having so much fun. Instead, she's defiant and she's angry and she clearly thinks that somehow she'll break free and make me suffer. Maybe her whole life has been about kicking back and finding a way to survive. Maybe she did pretty well at that before. But tonight, she's not going to go anywhere. Tonight she's finally met a fate she can't dodge.

"I want a razor-blade," I say finally, causing the girl to struggle once more against her restraints. "It doesn't have to be big. In fact, I think a smaller one might be better. I can be more... accurate."

I run my finger up the side of her face as tears run down her cheeks.

A moment later, I feel a nice, small razor-blade being placed in my right hand, and I hold it up for her to see.

She struggles again, with such force this time that the chair seems to be at risk of coming loose from its bolts.

“This is going to hurt,” I explain, “and it's going to last for as long as possible. But that won't be any fun if you still have that thing in your mouth.”

Reaching around, I loosen the knot at the back of her head, and then I pull the gag away.

“Help me!” she screams, as blood sprays from her mouth. “Somebody help me!”

“Who do you think is coming?” I ask calmly, as I turn the razor-blade around between my fingers. “There's no-one out there. No-one cares. But don't worry, I'll save your eyes for last. I want to see them as I'm doing all the other things.”

I hold the razor-blade out and set its edge against her left nipple.

“I'll kill you!” she snarls, pulling harder than ever against the restraints. “When I get out of here, I'll kill you!”

“You won't be getting out of here,” I reply, with the faintest twitch of a smile. “Didn't you realize that yet? You have no chance of leaving this place. I think they even dispose of your body parts here at the hotel.” I lean closer to her. “Welcome to Hotel Necro!”

I look down at the razor-blade, and then I start very slowly running its edge against the nipple. When that doesn't work, I realize that I need to press harder, so I try again. Even now, the blade doesn't actually break through, despite the fact that the nipple is fairly large and hard. I turn the blade around and try for a third time, pressing harder, but still it doesn't slice.

"You need to press more," Jason says, and I turn to see that he's watching from nearby. "Go quicker too."

"No!" Maria snarls. "I won't let you!"

I look back at the blade, but some part of me is holding back. I've tried to cut three times now, and each time I just don't seem able to press hard enough. I take a deep breath and try to pull myself together, and then I try yet again. Still, however, the razor-blade merely runs harmlessly against the nipple's edge.

"Here."

Suddenly Jason takes hold of my hand and flicks it against the woman's breast, and I watch in horror as her nipple is sliced open, causing her to scream.

"See?" Jason continues, letting go of my hand as blood flows down the breast. "It's not so hard, not really. Why don't you practice on the other one?"

I look at Maria, and suddenly she spits in

my face. I pull away and wipe the saliva from my cheek, and when I look at my hand I see that there's blood smeared across the side.

"Hey, bitch," Jason says, stepping past me and slamming his fist into Maria's jaw. "Do you wanna try that again?"

She starts sobbing, and now her body is shaking as she slumps back in the chair.

"Try doing it somewhere else, then," Jason says, taking my hand and guiding it down until it's between Maria's legs. He seems flustered, and a little angry. "Build up to the big stuff. There's no harm in that."

He lets go, and I turn the blade around and press it against the inside of Maria's left thigh. I know that if I run the blade slowly against her skin, I won't have much luck, so I take a deep breath and then I try to slash her skin. Even this doesn't work, however, and I'm starting to feel as if some part of me – the screaming, horrified part of me – is getting stronger. Is it possible that the pills are starting to wear off? Or is the 'real' me fighting back?

"Honey," Jason says, taking my hand again, "really, you need to be more forceful. Like this."

He slashes my hand against Maria's thigh, and I feel the blade dig deep into her flesh and then slice a bloodied line all the way to her wrecked knees.

"Help me!" she screams. "Somebody get me

out of here!”

Jason chuckles.

I take a deep breath and watch as blood runs from the wound on Maria's leg, pooling briefly on the chair before starting to dribble down onto the floor.

“Why don't you go a little further in?” Jason asks, nudging my arm. “I told you she's whored herself out, right? She should be used to people touching her down there.”

I look at Maria's vagina, but second by second I'm feeling as if I have to stop doing what I'm doing. I can feel a wave of panic in my chest, but at the same time the panic is somewhat dulled. I think I'm caught in two worlds, with my true self starting to win the fight against the self that came down here to kill. I wait, trying to decide what to do, but after a moment I realize that I really only have one choice. One of my two halves is winning the battle.

“Katie?” Jason says cautiously. “What are you waiting for?”

“I...”

I hesitate.

I need to play for time.

“A knife,” I stammer finally, turning to him and holding the razor-blade out. “I want a knife instead. A big one.”

“What for?”

"You'll see."

He stares at me for a moment, before shrugging and taking the razor-blade. As he heads back over to the table, I turn to Maria again and I try desperately to come up with some kind of plan.

"I'm going to get you out of here," I want to whisper, but I don't dare. After all, I have no idea how many microphones and cameras are dotted around this room, and I can't risk being overheard.

I need a plan.

I need to be smart.

I need to figure out how I'm going to get Maria out of here, without us both being killed.

"How about this one?" Jason asks, and I turn to see that he's brought a large, serrated knife over to me. "Think that'll do the job? Exactly what are you planning to do, anyway?"

I stare at the knife, and I can feel vital seconds slipping away.

"Katie? What's wrong?"

"Nothing," I reply, and I slowly reach out and take the knife. "There are just so many options, that's all," I add as I look up at my husband. "It's difficult to pick just one."

I could use the knife against Jason and force him to help me. The two of us might have a chance of fighting our way out of this place. Maria would slow us down, but we'd have to take her with us, and then we'd have to hope that we can get outside and call for help. Then again, I'm sure this place has a lot of security, and I'm by no means convinced that the police would be on our side. What if these Hotel Necro people have friends in high places? The fact that they're able to get away with this stuff means that they must have some serious protection.

"Just go with your gut instinct," Jason says.

The second option would be to try finding Doctor Strickland. I don't know if he's the ultimate boss of this place, but a knife against his throat might be enough to get him to let us go. I don't know what we'd do once we were out of the hotel, but we could worry about that later. I'd just have to scream and attract a lot of attention, and then people would realize what was happening. Then it'd just be a matter of spreading the news about this sick place as quickly and as far as possible.

"What are you waiting for?" Jason asks.

Option three is more extreme. I could just say that I want to keep Maria alive for a few more hours, and then I could try to sneak away. If there's some kind of back door to this place, I might be able to get out of the building and go to fetch help. I guess I'd just have to trust the police, but I'm sure Hotel Necro isn't *that* powerful and all-seeing. Is it? At some point I have to trust someone. Then again, I keep coming back to that earlier thought about all the powerful connections that these people must have. There must be a reason why they've been able to stay hidden for so long.

"Katie? Why are you waiting?"

"I'm not," I reply, before turning back to Maria and holding the knife up.

"I'm going to kill you!" she sneers, with pure anger in her voice. "You think you've got me, but I'm gonna rip your heart out!"

I move the tip of the blade onto her chest, while hoping that Jason will think I'm simply taking my time. I have three plans and I need to just pick one of them. My mind is racing, however, and I feel paralyzed by indecision. Why can't I just decide?

"You can totally do this," Jason says, stepping up closer behind me and reaching down to hold my wrist. "Don't hold back, Katie. Forget about all your inhibitions, all your ideas of what's right and what's wrong. Access your deepest, most primal desires."

The knife's tip is still pressing against Maria's chest.

"You dumb bitch," she says firmly. "Wait until I get out of this thing. You're dead!"

"I..."

My voice trails off.

I need a plan.

Now.

"Okay," Jason says after a moment, "I tell you want... I'll help you."

I open my mouth to reply, but suddenly he

forces my hand forward, driving the knife straight into Maria's chest and plunging it through her heart. I feel the blade scrape against her ribs, and I stare in horror at the knife's handle as I hear Maria let out a shocked gasp.

Looking at her face, I see that her eyes are wide open and her bottom lip is trembling. For the first time since I saw her tonight, she's no longer struggling against the restraints. She tries to say something, but then I feel Jason twisting my hand, forcing the knife to turn until the blade once again scrapes against her ribs. Finally, a faint gurgle erupts from Maria's lips and a line of blood starts running from her mouth and down over her chin.

“I know what you were planning,” Jason whispers very quietly into my ear. “I just saved your life, Katie.”

THIRTY-THREE

OPENING MY EYES, I see the ceiling of the hotel room. I blink, surprised by a crack of light that's running across my field of vision, and then I hear a snorting sound nearby.

Turning to my left, I see that Jason is fast asleep.

I sit up, and I immediately wince as I feel a flicker of pain in my head. I feel pretty dazed, as if I've barely slept at all, and for a moment I'm not entirely sure what happened. The last thing I remember is coming to bed and -

No.

No, I remember something else.

Suddenly it all comes rushing back. The rooms beneath the hotel. The blades. Michelle's smile, and Dan with the figure on the rack.

And Maria.

In my mind's eye, I replay that final moment over and over again, and I remember the feel of the blade slicing straight through her heart. Everything after that is a blur, but I vaguely remember Jason leading me out of the room and whispering to me that I had to stay quiet. After that...

After that, I think I was given another pill, something designed to knock me out. I remember Doctor Strickland telling me that I'd wake up in a few hours' time with no recollection of anything that had happened. He asked me if I'd enjoyed torturing and killing Maria, and I told him that I had. I asked him what would happen to her body, and he mentioned something about a furnace. I'd still been under the influence of the medication at that point, whereas now...

Now I remember everything.

I turn and look at Jason, but he's still asleep. Overcome by a sudden sense of shock, I clamber out of the bed and hurry through to the bathroom. I shut and lock the door, and then I turn and slide down to the floor. I want to scream, but somehow I manage to hold back. I clamp my hands over my mouth, holding the scream inside as I start sobbing.

I was completely heartless.

I didn't care about killing any of those people last night.

I even enjoyed it a little, at least at first.

Putting my head in my hands, I let out a pained, silent scream that feels as if it lasts forever. It's as if my entire body is about to shake apart, filled with rage and grief. I spent several hours down there in the basement of Hotel Necro and – while I felt little to no guilt or horror at the time – now all of those emotions are coming flooding into my system. I skipped the oblong pill because I wanted to remember, because I thought I had a duty to know exactly what happened at this place. Now, I'd give anything to have all these memories go away.

How can I ever live with what I did last night?

“Katie?” Jason calls out suddenly. “Are you okay?”

Sniffing back tears, I get to my feet.

“I'm fine,” I reply, although my voice sounds anguished. I take a deep breath as I see my teary-eyed reflection in the mirror. “I'll be out in a minute.”

That's when I remember the cameras. Jason told me that there are cameras everywhere in the hotel, even here in the bathroom. I look around, but I don't see anything. Still, is it possible that someone just saw me having that mini-breakdown? If they did, they might realize that I remember everything. Then again, they might not be monitoring the footage in real-time; it might be more a case of storing events so that they can be watched later. In which case, I might still be safe. The most important thing is that I have to seem normal when we check out.

I head to the sink and wash my trembling hands, and I tell myself that I have to hold myself together until we get home.

You can do this, I tell myself. *You're going to get away from this place and then you're going to make sure that Hotel Necro gets shut down. You're going to make the place world-famous, and the people in charge are going to pay for their crimes*.

First, though, I need to be able to walk out the door without arousing suspicion. Without looking like I'm about to scream.

Looking down at my hands, I see that they're still shaking. I have to find a way to hold them still, so I focus on trying to calm down.

"Katie?" Jason says, and then he knocks on the door. "Are you gonna be much longer? It's just, I kinda really need to pee."

"Coming," I reply, and I'm shocked by the fact that I seem to be pulling myself together.

There'll be time to sob later. Right now, I'm going to leave Hotel Necro and I'm going to bring this whole horrific place crashing down.

Somehow, my hands stop shaking.

I dry my eyes, and then I open the door and head out into the room.

"Are you okay?" Jason asks.

"Very," I reply, forcing a smile. "What time do we need to leave for the airport?"

"Ten," he says, and he watches as I walk over to the wardrobe. "Are you *sure* you're okay?"

"I'm fine," I tell him, before glancing over my shoulder and seeing him standing in the doorway. "Didn't you say that you need to pee?"

"Sure," he replies, and he heads into the bathroom and shuts the door.

I take a deep breath, and then I open the wardrobe and start taking my suitcase out. I know that there are cameras watching my every move, and I can't take the risk that at some point someone from the hotel is going to take a look at the pictures and start watching me. That's the *best* case scenario right now. I need to appear completely calm and relaxed, and somehow I manage to do just that as I set my suitcase on one of the chairs. I never really had myself down as someone who could fake this kind of thing, but right now I'm doing pretty well. I'm surprising myself. Maybe there's a little of the pill still in my bloodstream.

One thing's certain, however. I saw at least three people die last night, and I'm going to make sure that they're the last people who ever suffer at Hotel Necro.

"So there's a car picking us up later," Jason says as he emerges from the bathroom. "Our flight's at three, but I figured we should get to the airport a little early. Don't worry, I've managed to book us into a nice little lounge, so we won't have to sit around in some noisy cafe with all the riff-raff.

He steps up behind me and kisses the back of my neck.

"What was that?" he asks after a moment.

"What was what?" I reply.

"You shuddered just now. When I kissed you."

"No, I didn't."

"I swear you did."

Even though I feel nauseous, I turn to him.

"You're imagining things," I say, before leaning closer and kissing him on the lips. I hate doing this, but right now it's all part of the deception. I need him to think that I'm fine.

"Wow," he says once I've pulled away from the kiss. "Are you sure you don't wanna go again before I take a shower?"

"We'll save that for when we get home," I tell him. "Go on, you shower first. I need to do some packing."

THIRTY-FOUR

"I TRUST YOUR STAY was enjoyable?" Henri says as he folds the itemized receipt and slips it into an envelope.

"It was great, thank you," Jason replies, before glancing at me. "Wasn't it, honey?"

"I think it's been the best vacation of my life," I lie, somehow managing to smile. I never knew I could be this good at putting on a front. Is the pill still working a little, or am I just this steely? "I hope we can come back again next year."

"We would of course be most happy to have you," Henri says, just as a car horn blares outside the front door. "And if I'm not very much mistaken," he adds, "I believe your ride is here. Do you need any help with your bags?"

"We're fine, thanks," Jason says. "Thanks

again. Hopefully we'll see you again soon."

"There is *one* more thing," Henri adds, sliding a card and a pen across the desk. "Would you mind filling out this brief survey? It's just so that we can try to be even better in the future. Our aim is to constantly improve the experience we provide for our guests."

Jason hesitates, and then he takes the pen. I desperately want us to get out of here, but I guess Jason's worried about arousing any suspicions.

"I don't see why not," he says stiffly, as he casts me a brief glance. "Don't worry, honey. This'll only take a moment."

Hearing footsteps, I turn just in time to see Dan carrying some suitcase outside, while Michelle stops and looks at the sculpture near the window. Realizing that Jason's going to be busy for a couple of minutes with the survey, I wander over to Michelle and stop next to her. For a moment we stand in silence, as I try to think of some way to start this conversation. But even if I find a way, what is it that I actually want to say?

"It's funny," she says finally, with a strange, faraway tone to her voice, "but I feel very rested after my stay here, even if I feel as if my sleep was... interrupted somehow."

I swallow hard.

My mouth feels so dry.

"Do you remember your dreams from the

past few nights?" I ask, keen to check whether she's aware of what we did down in the basement area.

"Dreams?" She stares at the sculpture for a moment, as if she's trying to remember. "I don't know. I feel as if I definitely had dreams. Big dreams. Important dreams. Dreams I should remember. At the same time, I don't remember what they were about, or what happened in them. It's like having lots of empty picture frames on the walls in part of my mind. Is that strange?"

"Maybe they were upsetting dreams," I suggest.

Is it possible for me to somehow *make* her remember? Even if that's possible, is it something I should do? I can't help but think that maybe I should let her have her peace.

"Then I suppose I shouldn't try to think about the dreams, should I?" she replies. "Not if they're upsetting. After all, if I don't remember them now, what good would come from forcing myself?"

"Maybe they're important," I suggest.

She turns to me, and I swear I can see a hint of sadness in her eyes. Even if she took all the pills during her stay, I'm sure that some fragment of a memory *must* still be in her mind somewhere. She was doing awful things last night, she was torturing and killing people. Is it really possible that she's going to go back to her normal life and carry on as if everything's fine?

Hearing a faint rattling sound, I look down and see that her hands are trembling slightly, causing her bracelets to shake. After a moment, however, she gets the trembling under control.

"That just happens sometimes," she tells me. "It has for years."

"When did you first come to Hotel Necro?" I ask.

"Oh, I'm not even sure anymore." She hesitates. "Can it really have been almost twenty years? Time really flies, doesn't it?"

"Darling?" Dan leans back inside. "The car's packed. Let's go."

"It was nice to meet you," Michelle says, shaking my hand. "I'm sorry we didn't get to talk more, I think it might have been... illuminating."

She turns and heads to the door, following her husband out, although at the last moment she glances back at me. For a fraction of a second, I wonder whether she might suddenly scream that she remembers everything, but she simply looks at me with desperately sad eyes and then she disappears from view.

"I'm done," Jason says stiffly, coming over to join me. "I'm sorry about that, but I thought I should... Well, you know. Best to do what they want."

"Let's go," I reply.

With that, we both start wheeling out cases

toward the door, although I can't help glancing over my shoulder and seeing that Henri is watching us leave. He offers a little wave, and I give him a faint smile before heading out after Jason.

Even though I'm out of the hotel, I won't feel entirely safe until I'm back on home soil.

THIRTY-FIVE

"A TWO HOUR DELAY," Jason says with a sigh as he looks up at the board in the terminal building. "Great. I guess we should just go through to the lounge."

He turns to me.

"I hope you brought a good book," he adds, "because we might be here for a while."

"Let's go," I say, turning and heading toward the security area.

"Are you sure you're okay?" he asks, hurrying after me. "You've seemed a little stiff all morning."

"I'm just tired."

"Didn't you sleep well?"

I glance at him, and for a moment I wonder whether he's testing me.

"Let's just get through security," I say with a sigh. "You know how I get at airports. They're always such stressful places, even at the best of times."

We walk on, heading toward the security screening area. After a moment, however, a man in a dark suit steps past us, and we briefly making eye contact. I keep walking for a few more paces, and then I stop and turn to watch the man heading away.

"Honey?" Jason says cautiously. "What is it?"

"Nothing," I reply as the man disappears into the crowd, "it's just..."

My mind is racing, but deep down I already know that I'm right. I hesitate, and then I turn to Jason as a flicker of fear bites into my gut.

"You're going to think that I'm crazy," I tell him, "but I think I just saw the barman from the hotel."

"The barman?"

"From the bar downstairs," I continue, trying not to panic. "You know, the bar in the basement. I talked to him last night, just for a few minutes, and I swear he just walked past us."

Jason hesitates, but I already know that the man will be lost in the crowd by now.

"Why would he be here?" I ask. "Jason? Is this a bad sign?"

"No," he replies, but I can tell that he's

worried. “You might be wrong, Katie, there are so many -”

“I'm not wrong,” I say firmly. “It was him.”

“Sure, but -”

He stops suddenly, and then slowly he turns to me. There's a strange look in his eyes, as if he's been struck by some new realization.

“How do you even *remember* the barman?” he asks.

I open my mouth to make an excuse, but in an instant I realize that I've just slipped up.

“Jason, I...”

“Damn it!” he hisses, grabbing me and pulling me aside, away from the crowd. “What did you do, Katie?”

“There's no way they can possibly know,” I tell him.

“What did you do?”

“I skipped the oblong pill!” I snap. “I remember everything!”

“How did you skip it?” he asks. “This doesn't make any sense. I saw you swallow them both last night!”

“I managed to keep it in my mouth,” I reply, “and I spat it out in bed, but no-one can possibly have seen. I needed to know what was happening, Jason. I felt so cold and blank while we were doing those things to those people, I felt as if I wasn't really myself. But it *was* me, wasn't it? I tortured

Maria! I killed her! But if I didn't remember that, then I don't think I'd be so determined to expose the truth about that place!"

"I can't believe you'd be so stupid," he says, as he looks around to check that nobody's listening to us. "I told you what you had to do, Katie! I told you to take the pills and to just get through the night. It was simple!"

"I had to know!" I say firmly. "I had to remember what I did!"

"And what now, huh?" he asks. "Do you feel better for knowing?"

"I'm going to bring that place down," I tell him. "That's what matters."

He stares at me as if he can't quite believe what I'm saying.

"When we get back to New York," I continue, "I'm going to expose Hotel Necro and all the terrible things that happen there. I don't care what you think, Jason, I refuse to ignore what they're doing. They're murdering people! *We* murdered people and it's been going on for years! How many people have died?"

"You don't get it," he replies. "Do you seriously think they'll let this happen?"

"Once we get to America, they can't stop us!"

"Where did you put the pill?"

"What do you mean?"

"After you spat it out, what did you do with it?"

"I tucked it down between the bed and the wall."

"And then what?"

"They won't find it," I tell him, although I'm starting to realize that I should have retrieved the pill this morning. The past few hours have been so crazy, and maybe I haven't quite managed to get my thoughts straight. "Not before we get out of here, at least. Will they?"

"And you didn't do anything suspicious after you woke up?" he asks.

"Like what?"

"Anything, Katie! Anything that might make them realize that you broke the rules of that place!"

For a moment, I think back to my breakdown in the bathroom.

"We have to get out of here," he says, grabbing my hand and leading me across the terminal building, heading toward the exit. "They're obviously onto us. You have no idea who you're messing with, Katie. This is an international organization with links in every country. They're ruthless when it comes to shutting down anything or anyone that might blow their cover, and they have actual governments on their side."

"You're acting as if they're above the law!

Let's just get on the plane and -"

"There's no way we're getting on that plane," he says as we hurry outside and head toward the taxi rank. "We'll leave our bags there, that should mean it takes longer for them to realize that we're skipping town."

"Where are we going?"

"Away from here. Somewhere. Anywhere. I'll book us some fresh tickets from another airport once we're on the way." He stops at a taxi and leans down to speak to the driver. "How much to take us to Geneva?" He takes his wallet from his pocket and pulls out a wad of notes. "Five hundred euros," he continues, reaching into the car. "Geneva! Will you take us?"

The driver says something in Italian.

Jason hands him the cash and then opens the rear door.

"Get in!" he says firmly.

"Jason," I stammer, "why don't we just -"

"Get in the goddamn taxi!" he snaps, while looking around as if he's worried that at any moment we'll be spotted. "It's our only shot! They'll be looking for us here in Turin, at least for now. That should give us enough time to get over the border to Switzerland, and then we just have to pray that they don't track us down until we're out of here. After that..."

His voice trails off, and for a moment he

seems utterly at a loss for words.

"After that," he adds, "I'll think of something. I don't know what, but something. Now get in the car!"

Shocked by the urgency in his voice, I climb in, and he immediately slams the door shut. I'm trembling with fear, but at the same time I figure that I just need to listen to Jason and wait until we're safely away from this city. I'm starting to realize that this Hotel Necro place is a *really* big deal, but at the same time I know I can't stop now. And as Jason takes his place beside me, and as the taxi pulls away and joins the flow of traffic, I tell myself that I just need to stay strong for a little longer.

Once we get home, everything will be alright. And I'm going to make sure that the whole world knows about the horrors of Hotel Necro.

THIRTY-SIX

THE RADIO ANNOUNCER CONTINUES to babble on as we drive along a country road. I tried asking the driver to turn the sound down, or to turn the radio off altogether, but I guess he didn't understand. Either that, or he just didn't care.

"We're booked on a new flight," Jason says after a moment, as he continues to tap at his phone. "We leave from Geneva tonight. Hopefully we'll be in the air before they're able to track us down."

"So we'll be back home soon?" I reply.

"If everything goes according to plan. We're relying on them not moving fast enough to catch us, but we might get lucky." He checks something else on his phone. "What the..."

"What's wrong?" I ask.

He hesitates, before tilting the phone so that

I can see the screen. I see a video of a plane on a runway with smoke coming from its engines, and I spot the headline on the news story.

"A plane was grounded?" I ask. "Where?"

"Where do you think?" he replies. "That's the plane we were supposed to be on, Katie. Apparently it suffered some kind of technical failure right before takeoff. Convenient, huh? Obviously some important people were still worried that we might somehow use that flight to get away."

"No," I reply, shaking my head, unable to believe that any of this is possible, "that can't be right. It has to be a coincidence."

"At least they didn't just blow it up," he says. "I wouldn't put anything past these people."

"They wouldn't do that," I tell him. "They *couldn't*! How could they take stop a whole plane from taking off, just to get to you and me?"

"These people don't know how to do things quietly," he replies. "I already told you, they have connections everywhere. Right now, our only chance is to outrun those connections. It'll take time for them to figure everything out. Even *these* people can't cover every airport in Europe, not simultaneously, so we just have to hope that we get lucky." He sighs. "Why couldn't you have just done what I asked, Katie? Why did you have to break the rules?"

"I wanted to do the right thing," I tell him,

as I struggle to hold back tears. "I wanted to help."

"Help who?"

"I don't know! Anyone! I thought I couldn't just walk away from all of this, I thought I could put it all right. What's happening at that place is monstrous. When I decided to come to Hotel Necro, I didn't really understand what I was getting myself into. I mean, I can't have done. I'm not the kind of person who'd want to get involved with something like this, am I?" I wait for an answer, but he's checking something on his phone. "*Am* I, Jason?"

"This isn't the way to Geneva," he mutters, as he examines a map. "We're heading in totally the wrong direction."

"Are you sure?"

He glances at me, and I can see that he's worried.

"My friend," he says, leaning forward and tapping the driver on the shoulder, "I want you to drive us toward -"

Suddenly the car speeds up, and a clicking sound indicates that the doors are being locked.

"He's taking us out into the middle of nowhere!" Jason says, clearly starting to panic. "This is an ambush!"

"How?" I ask. "They couldn't have set this up so fast!"

"Looks like they did," he replies, before lunging forward and grabbing the driver, trying to pull him away from the wheel. "I'm sorry, buddy," he continues, "but I'm afraid I need to take over!"

The car skids across the road, first one way and then the other, as Jason and the driver fight for control. Realizing that we're in danger of crashing, I try to get my safety belt undone so that I can help Jason, but at that moment the car spins wildly and slides straight off the road, hitting a ditch before starting to roll. The windshield shatters, showering us all with glass. I scream as I'm tipped upside down, and the car rolls several more times before finally coming to a rest on its roof. The whole violent event is over in less than half a minute.

For a moment, hanging upside down, I remain completely still. I have no idea what to do, but a moment later I hear an agonized cry.

Looking over at the driver, I see that he's struggling with his legs, which appear to have been crushed as the front part of the car was damaged. There's blood on his hands, and he lets out another cry as he tries desperately to get free.

Turning to Jason, I see that he's trying to get out from the belt that's holding him in place. I reach over and help, and he does the same for me, and then we manage to get one of the side doors open. As the driver continues to gasp in pain, I follow Jason out of the car, and then he helps me stumble to my feet.

"They're everywhere!" he gasps, limping

slightly as he leads me away from the overturned vehicle. “We have to get as far away from Turin as possible.”

“We have to go to the police!” I tell him. “We need help!”

“We can't trust the police. They'd probably just hand us straight back over to those bastards.”

“If we can't trust the police, what are we supposed to do?”

“First we need to survive,” he replies, “and *then* we can figure out where we're going to get help. We'll be -”

Stopping suddenly, he looks past me, as if something concerning has caught his eye.

I turn and see a small dot in the sky, and at that moment I realize I can hear the distant hum of a small plane getting closer. I tell myself that this can't be anything to do with us, and then I remember that old film with the guy being chased by bad guys in a plane.

“That can't be them as well, can it?” I ask, taking a step back. “Jason, there's no way...”

“Get down!”

He pulls me away from the vehicle, and we duck down in the ditch. Looking up, I watch as the plane flies toward us. I keep telling myself that this situation is surreal, that none of this can actually be happening. And then, just as I start to wonder which way we should run, the plane veers off to one side and heads away, finally disappearing into the distance. I keep waiting for it to return, but finally the distant hum is no more.

"It wasn't them?" I ask, turning to Jason.

"Maybe not," he replies, as we get to our feet and clamber back out of the ditch, "but we still need to be careful. Katie, I -"

Suddenly a gunshot rings out and Jason collapses.

Shocked, I turn just as the taxi driver aims at me. He pulls the trigger, but this time the gun only clicks impotently. He tries again, and then he throws the gun in a rage. Still trapped in the wreckage, he lets out a cry of anger.

"Jason!" I gasp, dropping to my knees and rolling him over, only to find that there's a bloodied wound on his chest, close to his heart.

He tries to say something, but there's already blood running from one corner of his mouth.

"It's going to be okay!" I tell him, as I try to figure out what to do next. "I'm going to get help!"

He reaches up and grabs my shoulder, and then he pulls me closer.

"I love you," he gurgles, barely able to get the words out. "Katie, you have to run and *keep* running. Promise me you'll get as far from here as..."

His voice trails off.

"I'm not leaving you!" I sob.

"You've got to get away!" he says, as he pulls his wallet from his pocket and slides it into my hand. "Take out cash, use cash as much as possible. Get to another country and take a flight home, as fast as you can. Then you have to keep your head down! You have to hide!"

"I can't do that!" I tell him. "This madness has to end!"

"Promise me!" he gasps, reaching up and touching the side of my face. "You're all that matters to me now, Katie. I love you so much, I always have. You're the best person I've ever met. You have such a good soul, never let anyone ruin that. I'm just so sorry that I..."

He hesitates, and then he lets out a long, slow gasp.

"No!" I shout, shaking him hard. "Jason! Come back!"

I set him flat against the ground and check for a pulse, but his heart doesn't seem to be beating.

"Jason!" I yell, shaking him again. "Don't leave me! Jason! I need you!"

THIRTY-SEVEN

THE ONLY SOUND COMES from my own feet, half walking and half dragging as I stumble along this endless, desolate road. I'm in the middle of nowhere, several miles now from the car's wreckage, and I feel as if I'm going to collapse at any moment.

Once I realized that Jason was dead, I just wanted to curl up and die right next to him. In some ways, I think that would have been the better option. Instead, however, I somehow managed to get to my feet. I checked the car and found that the driver had passed out, probably due to all the blood that he'd lost. He might even have been dead, but I didn't check. Maybe I should have pulled him from the vehicle and beaten him for what he did to Jason, but somehow I lacked the energy.

And Jason's words were ringing in my ears then, as they ring in my ears now:

"You've got to get away! Get to another country and take a flight home, as fast as you can. Then you have to keep your head down! You have to hide!"

So here I am, shuffling along a barren road, with not even a plan for what I'm going to do next. I know that I have to run, that I have to get away from this madness, but the shock of Jason's death has left me in a kind of daze. It's as if, deep down, I'm too scared to feel anything. I can only think about Jason, and about the fact that I didn't have time to say much before he died.

I didn't even tell him how much I loved him.

Suddenly, hearing a distant humming sound, I turn and see that a car is coming this way. I stop and watch as it come closer, and finally the vehicle pulls up next to me. There's a family inside, or at least I assume that they're a family. There's a man at the wheel and a woman next to him, and a little boy in the back seat.

"Are you okay?" the woman asks cautiously, as the car's engine continues to run.

"I..."

I hesitate, before reminding myself that I have to keep going. For Jason.

"I need to get to an airport," I tell them. "Any airport. *Almost* any airport."

"Well," she replies, "we're on our way to Nice. There's an airport there." She pauses. "Can we give you a ride?"

I hear a faint, muffled murmur coming from her husband. I think he's trying to get her to change her mind, and I don't blame him. I probably look pretty rough and crazy, standing here at the side of the road, and the boy in the back seat is staring at me as if he's a little scared.

"Did something happen to you?" the woman asks.

I swallow hard.

How could I even begin to explain? They'd think that I'm crazy, they'd probably take me straight to the nearest police station. Hell, that's probably what I'd do if our roles were reversed.

"A ride to the airport would be cool," I say finally, even though I feel bad for interrupting these people. I just need to move faster. "Thank you."

I open one of the doors and climb into the car, and there's an awkward silence as I pull the door shut and wait for us to get moving. I'm very much aware that the kid is uncomfortable, and that the husband is angry at his wife for inviting me. Still, he starts the car again, and I tell myself that everything will be fine so long as I can just get home. That's all that matters now. I need to get home and then figure out a way to let the world know about Hotel Necro.

"We're on vacation," the woman says, turning and smiling at me. "We're from Wakefield, Virginia, but we're here to see Europe for six weeks." She pauses. "This is going to sound strange," she adds after a moment, "but have we met before? I can't place it, but you look kinda familiar."

"I... No," I say, trying to seem as normal as possible. "I don't think we have."

"Huh." She stares for a few seconds more, and she seems really convinced that she recognizes me. "I guess you must just have one of those faces."

"I guess I must."

"So are you lost or something?" she asks. "This road doesn't seem like it really goes to or from anywhere major. To be honest, we only came along this way because we got lost."

"We didn't get lost," her husband says.

"We got lost," she says with a smile.

"My car broke down," I tell her, but in my mind's eye all I can see is the sight of Jason's dead body. I want to scream, but I don't dare. My husband died in my arms and I can't even tell anyone. Not yet.

"Huh." She pauses again. "So, at the airport..."

"It's a rental," I reply, and again I'm surprised by how good I am at this lying business. "I'll tell them. They can go get it."

"That's cool. I guess it's their fault if the thing died under you."

"I guess."

She stares at me, as if she has a million other questions, and then she turns and looks ahead as her husband silently drives us along the road. I'm pretty sure that even the wife is having a few regrets now. Sure enough, a moment later I catch my own reflection in one of the mirrors, and I see that I look pretty rough. At least there's no blood on me.

"Do you mind if I put the radio on?" the woman asks finally.

"Go for it," I reply, relieved at the thought of having something to fill the silence.

She switches the radio on, and some kind of rock music starts blaring from the speakers. That's fine by me, because it helps to drown out the thoughts that are rushing through my head. I feel as if I'm on pause, as if I've had to freeze all my emotions. They're still there, waiting to burst out once I'm safe, but right now I have to keep them contained. I'm not safe yet, but once I get home I'm going to find a way to make the world see what's happening at Hotel Necro. That's all I care about now.

THIRTY-EIGHT

"THANK YOU," I SAY again as I step back from the car. "You've been so helpful."

"Have a good trip!" the woman replies, but her husband is already easing the car away from the side of the road, rejoining the traffic. He seems to be in quite a hurry.

I've got a feeling that they're going to be having a conversation about picking up weirdos from the side of the road.

Turning, I start making my way toward the airport's departure hall.

***

"Passenger Leyton Jones, traveling on flight WA015 to Athens, please make yourself known to staff at the Wellingford Air desk. That's passenger Leyton Jones to the Wellingford Air desk, please."

"This is your gate number," the woman says as she slides my boarding pass toward me, with the number 15 circled in pen, "and you should be boarding at around half seven."

"Thank you," I reply, trying to hide the fact that I'm surprised to get this far. I booked the ticket on my phone, during the drive here, and I'm still worried that the Hotel Necro people will somehow track me down. I guess one slight advantage might be that I used my own card, whereas James used his to pay for the whole trip. It might be the case that Hotel Necro's friends have yet to get all my details into their system.

"You have fast-track security access," the woman continues, "and you'll find the Concordia lounge on the first floor once you're through. Have a great flight!"

"Thank you," I say again, and I take the boarding pass before turning and walking away.

***

As I stand in the queue at security, I can't help glancing around, looking out for any sign that I'm being watched. I'm sure I look a little suspicious right now, but that's fine. I don't mind being questioned by any of the actual staff here. I just need to make sure that no-one from Hotel Necro is lurking.

"M'am?" the guy on the other side of the metal detector says. "Your turn."

I force a smile and step forward, while trying to look as boring and inconspicuous as possible.

***

"I love you. Katie, you have to run and keep running."

That's what Jason said to me, as he lay dying on the ground near the wrecked car. I keep replaying his words over and over, terrified that I might soon forget the sound of his voice.

And then there's the driver of the taxi, the man who pulled the trigger and shot my husband. Why didn't I do anything to him? Why didn't I go over there and make him pay? For a moment, I feel pure rage rising through my body, but I quickly realize that I did the best thing. I got away from there, and now I'm so close to getting home. All I need to do now is get on the plane.

A couple of police officers wander past, carrying guns. I briefly consider going over to them and telling them everything, but then I tell myself that I can't trust them. I can't trust anyone, not yet. Not until I get back to America. Even then, I'm not sure where to go first.

***

7pm. Half an hour to go before we're supposed to get on the plane.

I feel as if I need to scream, but I've waited this long so I guess I can wait a little longer. Still, sitting here in this waiting area is driving me crazy, so I get to my feet and head off to find a restroom.

***

Pushing the door open, just as a woman slips past me on her way out, I head over to the sinks. I need some water on my face, I need to wake myself up a little.

Looking down at my hands, I see that they're still not trembling. I don't know how I'm managing to hold myself together.

"Good evening, Ms. Johnson."

Startled, I spin around and see Doctor Strickland standing behind me. He reaches over and turns a dial on the door, locking it to stop anyone else coming through.

"What a long way you've come to take your flight home," he says with a faint smile. "I've come a long way too. I wanted to see you personally, rather than sending some heavy-handed oaf. At

Hotel Necro, we pride ourselves on the personal touch."

I look around, trying to spot something I can use as a weapon.

"I'm truly sorry about your husband," Doctor Strickland continues, "but he was very much aware of the rules that we have in place at Hotel Necro. These were emphasized to him yesterday, and the day before, when we first began to realize that you were perhaps having... difficulties... sticking to those rules."

I need to think.

I need a plan.

"You're not in any danger here," he says. "I've simply come to fetch you. We're going to go back to the hotel, and we're going to have a little talk. At Hotel Necro, we always try to do the right thing. This isn't the first time that a guest's experience has gone a little awry, but we've always found a way to resolve matters in the past and I'm confident that we can do so again."

"You killed Jason," I reply through gritted teeth.

Come on, Katie. Think!

"And I've expressed my genuine regret for that," he replies. "There are really two ways we can do this. The first is that you can come with me calmly, without a struggle. You have my word that I'm here alone. We sent one person to each of the major airports, and I just happen to have been the one who came to Nice. The second option is that you can struggle, and then I'll have to get creative. Either way, the outcome will be the same. You're coming with me."

I shake my head.

"You *are*," he says firmly. "You might not remember, but both you and your husband explicitly signed an agreement before you arrived at the hotel, confirming that you understood what would happen in this kind of situation."

"I signed an agreement saying that you'd kill my husband?" I ask, as I feel white hot rage building in my chest.

"Not in quite those terms," he replies, "but basically, yes."

Staring at him, I realize that he's serious. I could scream and try to get attention that way, but something tells me that he'll have that angle covered. I could go with him and then try to run but, again, this guy's clearly no fool. At the same time, I have no weapon, I have no way at all of fighting back, and I can't help but notice that Doctor Strickland's right hand keeps touching something in his jacket pocket. I have no doubt that he could get a gun through security. After all, he seems to be able to do just about anything he wants.

"Let's not dilly-dally," he says finally. "Time's ticking, Ms. Johnson. You *are* going to do the right thing, aren't you?"

"The right thing?" I swallow hard, as I realize that I only have one chance here. "Sure. I'm going to do *exactly* the right thing."

I step forward, making my way over to the door.

"That's good," he says, reaching out to turn the dial. "For a moment there, I was worried you might -"

Before he can finish, I throw myself at him, slamming hard into his chest. He grabs me by the shoulders and swings me around, but I was expecting that. I slam my knee into his groin, and he lets out an anguished gasp as I grab the back of his jacket's collar and throw him forward. Keeping hold of him, I slam his head against the edge of the sink, hoping to knock him out, but he manages to twist around and kick my legs out from under me.

I fall, but I bring him down too.

Slamming into the floor, I pull aside to avoid having him land on me, and then I turn and try to punch him. He ducks out of the way and then he grabs me by the throat, immediately squeezing hard and digging his thumbs into my flesh as hard as he can. I wriggle for a moment, trying to get free, and then I summon some strength from somewhere and throw him back against the wall. He lets out a pained grunt. Before he can grab me again, I slam my shoulder against his chest, but at that moment I see that he's pulled a gun from his pocket.

I grab his wrist, keeping him from aiming at me.

"You're making a fatal mistake!" he sneers.

I try to pull the gun from his hand, but he's holding on too tight. For a moment, I'm not sure what to do, but then I realize that I've still got one good chance. I turn to him and see the anger in his eyes, and then I headbutt him as hard as I can, hitting his nose and immediately feeling a crunching sensation.

Turning, I see that he's let go of the gun, which is now sliding across the floor. I scramble over to grab the damn thing, but at the last second Strickland grabs my ankle and holds me back.

"You could have been on your way home by now!" he snarls. "You could have been enjoying all the benefits of your stay!"

I'm still reaching for the gun, but my fingertips are falling just a few inches short.

"All you had to do was take your pills," he continues, as he starts pulling himself toward me. "All you had to do was take your goddamn medication!"

I gasp as I try again to reach the gun. I'm closer, but still not close enough.

"But you had to be a hero, didn't you?" Strickland says, grabbing my shoulders and trying to pull me back. "Well, let's see how that works out for you! You'll make a fetching victim for the next guests at Hotel Necro!"

Letting out an angry cry, I lunge forward, and by some miracle I manage to grab the gun. I put my finger against the trigger, and then I turn and aim the gun straight at Strickland's bloodied face.

He freezes.

"You wouldn't!" he sneers.

I adjust my grip. For a moment, I actually consider shooting this man at point blank range. Would that be any worse, any more cowardly, than what his henchman did to Jason? I could blast this asshole's head all over the wall. Then I could explain, and no amount of dishonesty or corruption would be able to sweep the truth about Hotel Necro under the carpet.

I begin to squeeze the trigger.

And then, suddenly, I remember another thing that Jason said to me as he was dying:

"I love you so much, I always have. You're the best person I've ever met. You have such a good soul, Katie. Never let anyone ruin that."

"Give me the gun," Strickland says firmly. "I think you'll find that that's your best, and only, option right now."

I stare at him for a moment longer.

"Now!" he screams.

"Okay," I say finally, and I turn the gun around in my hands.

He smiles.

Suddenly I slam the gun's handle against the side of his head, as hard as I can, and he lets out a stunned groan as he slumps down. I hold the gun up, ready to hit him again, but he doesn't move. I wait, in case this is a trick, and then finally I realize that I actually *have* managed to knock him out.

“I think you'll find,” I say breathlessly, “that that's called pistol-whipping.”

I scramble to my feet and grab his arms, and I drag him into one of the cubicles. Once I've set him on the floor, I head back out and drop the gun into the bin. I check myself in the mirror, and I realize that fortunately I still don't have any obvious signs of blood. My heart is racing and I feel as if I still need to scream, but I've come this far and I'm not going to stop now.

I'm going home, and then I'm going to expose Hotel Necro to the world.

Turning, I glance at Strickland's unconscious body as I head to the door.

“Have fun when you wake up, asshole,” I mutter. “Pretty soon, Hotel Necro's gonna be closed for business. On the bright side, you're gonna be famous.”

I step outside. Conveniently, there's an Out of Order sign hanging on the door to one of the other restrooms, so I swap it over and then I start making my way to the gate.

With each step, I expect to feel a hand on my shoulder, to find that I'm going to be stopped. I look around, and every face seems as if it could be someone from Hotel Necro. Strickland said he'd come here alone, but is that possible? I guess he might have been telling the truth, but I'm still convinced that somehow something is going to get in my way. And yet, as I reach the gate and find that boarding has started, and as I join the queue and get my passport and boarding card ready, I can't shake a feeling of hope that maybe – just maybe – I'm going to get away from here after all.

The flight attendant looks at my passport and scans my boarding pass, and then she smiles as she wishes me a pleasant flight.

"Thanks," I reply, barely able to believe that this is working.

My heart is pounding as I step past her and head along the corridor that leads to the plane. All the sounds of the airport suddenly seem so loud, but I'm finally starting to believe that this is really possible.

I'm going home.

THIRTY-NINE

IT'S THE MIDDLE OF the night when I finally reach New York. I feel like a zombie as I make my way through the airport, but with each step I find that nothing bad happens. Maybe Hotel Necro's reach isn't long enough to reach me here. Maybe I'm really free.

Once I'm through immigration, I stop in the arrivals hall and look around. There's no-one here to meet me, of course, but the truth is that I barely dared plan for what I should do next. I can feel the scream still in my chest, still waiting to get out, but I know it's too soon for that. I have to stay calm for a little while longer, and after a moment I spot a police officer nearby.

Is he part of it all?

Is he working for Hotel Necro?

I can't assume that.

At some point, I have to trust somebody.

"Are you okay, M'am?" he asks as I head over to him.

"I..."

How do I say this?

"I need to talk to someone," I stammer finally. "Something happened, and I need to tell someone. I'm a... I think I'm a witness to something awful that happened while I was on vacation."

"Okay," he says cautiously, "are you in any danger?"

"No," I reply, before thinking for a moment. "I don't know. Maybe." There are tears in my eyes now. "They killed my husband."

He hesitates, and it seems from his expression that he understands something's very wrong. Maybe he believes what I'm telling him, or maybe he thinks I'm insane. He seems genuinely confused, though, and I'm pretty sure that he's not just a good actor.

"Why don't you come with me?" he says, with a friendly smile. "We'll see about finding the right person to assist you."

"Thank you," I reply, and I start following him along a corridor. "I don't even know where to begin."

"We have someone here you can talk to," he explains, "and they'll know who to put you in touch with." He stops at a door and scans a key-card, and then he gestures for me to go through. "After you, M'am. Please."

"Thank you," I reply, still feeling like a zombie as I head into the next room. "I just don't know where to begin. It's all going to sound totally incredible when I start."

"It'll all be okay," a familiar voice says suddenly.

I freeze.

"Welcome home," the voice adds, as the door shuts behind me.

For a moment, I don't dare believe that this can be happening. And then, slowly, I turn and see Jason sitting at a desk at the far end of the room.

FORTY

"YOUR NAME," JASON SAYS, as I sit on chair and stare at him, "is not Katie Johnson. Katie Johnson doesn't exist. Your name is Elizabeth Bell Langley and you're the CEO of Dupatroyn, a tech and pharmacy company based in Seattle. You're personally worth more than five billion dollars."

I don't know what to say.

All I can do is stare at him and wait for this madness to start making sense.

"I'm dreaming," I whisper. "I... I have to be dreaming."

"About a year ago," he continues, "you made the difficult decision to shut down one of the company's divisions. There were angry demonstrations. You decided to go and speak to the fired employees personally, but things got a little out of hand. They were yelling awful things at you, accusing you of being heartless and cruel. And then one of the employees, a man named Michael Duncan, physically assaulted you. He was pulled away quickly, but not before he managed to cut your face with a knife."

Reaching up, I touch the scar on my cheek.

This can't really be happening.

"At first, you seemed fine," Jason explains, "but over the following months I began to notice that something wasn't right. The attack had shaken you, and as your husband I began to notice that you were becoming withdrawn. I tried to talk to you about it, but you insisted you were fine. Things got worse and worse, however, and the Dupatroyn board became concerned about your continued ability to lead the company. Finally, you admitted to me that you'd begun to doubt yourself. The protesters had called you a heartless bitch. A monster. They'd said you were evil. And those word had dug into your soul like little daggers, Elizabeth. You'd begun to believe them."

I open my mouth to tell him that he's wrong, but somehow – deep down – I feel as if maybe all of this is true.

"That's when we decided to go to Hotel Necro," he says. "It's one of a number of full-immersion multi-day experiences, offered by a very exclusive company. You wanted to find out whether you're truly a good person at heart, so you went for the full package, which involves having your memory temporarily wiped. It's like a factory reset of your personality, for a day or two, to see who you really are. The Hotel Necro package involves a kind of horror thriller story-line in which you gradually uncover bad things at a mysterious hotel. Think of it as like a psychological escape room, but thousands of times more realistic. And bigger. And the room, in this case, was actually your own sense of self-loathing."

"Hotel Necro isn't real?" I stammer, with tears in my eyes.

"It really exists, but it's not quite what you thought it was."

"It's some kind of escape room?"

"The experience was tailored for you," he explains. "Full immersion means *full* immersion, Elizabeth. The people who died there really died. It wouldn't work any other way. For example, Maria was a homeless girl who was paid to attack you in the street. She didn't know what would happen to her after, of course, but Hotel Necro is very experienced at this sort of thing. They created a story for you to experience, so that you could see how you'd react. And you passed with flying colors, Elizabeth. You fought back, and you did the right thing. I mean, who *wouldn't* want to be the plucky heroine in a good old-fashioned horror story?"

"The pills..."

"You were always supposed to uncover the truth about that place," he replies. "Various scenarios were set up so that you'd do that, and so that it would feel natural. If you hadn't skipped that pill, you'd have found out some other way. The point is that, when push came to shove, you did the right thing. I mean..." He chuckles. "You have to admit, the whole thing was a little corny. It was designed to be like one of those gory horror movies, and you were set up to be the heroine. I think, by any standards, you excelled. The people at Hotel Necro gave you almost full marks. You should feel really pleased with yourself."

Swallowing hard, I try to take all of this in, but it's too much.

"There were a couple of moments when I thought maybe you'd realize something was off," he adds. "Did you notice that, when we checked in, the guy on the desk looked at your fake passport and called you Katie? The passport listed your name as Catherine, so he should have said that version of it instead. There were a few other little errors like that, but overall nothing that seemed to leap out at you and really threaten the illusion."

Jason gets to his feet and steps around the desk, coming over to me.

"I'm so proud of you," he says. "I've got to admit, I think I was pretty good as well. I never thought I could act, but my death scene was pretty cool, huh? Don't you think?"

Looking up at him, I don't know what to say.

"This might help you understand," he says, taking his phone from his pocket and bringing up a video. "You were so conflicted, Elizabeth. I was really worried about you, before we decided to take the Hotel Necro package."

He starts the video, and I immediately see that it seems to be from the same session as the video he showed me the other day.

"Maybe I really am an awful person," Video Me says on the screen. "Maybe I'm a monster, maybe everything they shouted at me was true."

"You can't possibly believe that," Video Jason's voice says. "Elizabeth, please..."

"But how do I know?" Video Me sobs in response, sounding a little tinny thanks to the phone's speakers. "How can I ever be sure?"

"That's why we're doing this," Video Jason's voice replies. "We've picked the perfect package. The Hotel Necro story-line is going to really test you, but I know you have what it takes to be a heroine. To do the right thing. To fight through it all and come out stronger the other side. Maybe you don't have that faith in yourself, but I do. You're a good person. The ultimate aim of the Hotel Necro game is to make it all the way back here to New York, with the intention of exposing the truth. I know you'll do that."

"And I was right," Jason says now, as he stops the video. "The police officer out there was the final test, and you passed with flying colors. Everyone was amazed at how well you did. You needed very little prompting to let the story-line play out as it was intended. They told me that you were one of the best players they've ever had."

"I still don't know if this can be true," I reply, and my voice is trembling with shock. "I saw you die, Jason."

"Here," he replies, taking something from his pocket and holding it out to me. "You should take this."

Looking at the palm of his hand, I see a small, oblong blue pill.

"The effect of the red pills will wear off in a day or two," he says, "but this is what they call the Wake Up pill. It brings you back much more quickly. You'll still remember everything that happened at Hotel Necro, Elizabeth. You'll remember how you proved yourself. You'll understand that all those cruel comments were untrue."

I reach out and take the pill, and then Jason hands me a glass of water.

"It was all a set-up?" I say cautiously. "It was just a game?"

"It was a game with a purpose," he replies,

"and you scored 97%. You only dropped points for not trying to help the Michelle character, but she was just a side quest in the whole thing. You don't need to worry about that. When you were talking to her as we were leaving, you were technically supposed to offer to help her, but 97% is still amazing. It's higher than anyone else has ever scored in that particular game. Don't be too hard on yourself, honey. You did great."

"Michelle was an actress?"

He nods.

"But the people who died," I continue, "*they* were..."

"Don't think about that."

"But they really died!"

"The threat had to be real," he says firmly, "and they would have died anyway. Hotel Necro's pretty popular, someone plays it almost every weekend. If those people hadn't died in your game, they'd die in the next. We paid ten million dollars for the full Hotel Necro experience, Elizabeth, and I'd say we really got value for that money. Actually, to give it the proper name, the experience is called *Escape From Hotel Necro*. Now you can forget all those horrible things that people said to you. You can go back to being the strong, powerful, confident woman who built Dupatroyn up from nothing. And let me tell you, the board will be *very* pleased to have you back at the helm. They've been getting nervy, especially since the press started asking questions."

I stare at the pill.

"It's time, Elizabeth," Jason says calmly, as he places a hand on my shoulder.

I hesitate, and then I put the pill in my mouth and chase it down with some water.

"Just give it a few seconds," Jason continues, squeezing my shoulder. "You're about to remember your real life. You're about to come back."

He kisses me on the cheek.

"Game over."

EPILOGUE

Two weeks later...

"ELIZABETH! ELIZABETH, OVER HERE! How does it feel to be back at work? Do you think the board of Dupatroyn did a good job while you were away?"

"I think they did fabulously," I reply, flashing a smile as the cameras click and flash. I didn't expect to find so many reporters here in the lobby of the building, despite this being my first official day back at work. I guess my brief time out of the limelight must have attracted quite a lot of attention. "I've always said, I could never ask for a better team."

"There have been rumors that you were at a secret rehab facility in Europe, and that you were addicted to pain-killers. Can you comment on those rumors?"

I turn, just as the reporter thrusts a microphone toward me.

"I'm not going to comment on individual stories that have been circulating," I tell him, sticking to the linc that Jason and I worked out earlier. "All I'm prepared to say is that I was fully supported during a period of personal difficulty, and that I'm now back and raring to go."

"Elizabeth, over here!"

I turn and see another reporter trying to get my attention.

"My name's Katie Lewis, from the tech journal Instawarble. Do you have anything to say about plans to close any more divisions? There are rumors that you might be about to lay off some more employees."

"All our plans have been laid out in the open," I tell her, having expected some version of this question, "and I'm very happy with our current alignments. A small number of employees will be leaving us today, and then we anticipate continuing with our new arrangement until at least the third quarter next year." I turn to walk away, before hesitating for a moment as I stare at the woman. "That's a nice name, by the way," I add finally. "Katie. It's very sweet."

"This way," Jason says, nudging my arm.

"I'm sorry, everyone, but my wife really does have a lot to get done today. As I'm sure you're all aware, she's giving evidence in Washington on Monday before a congressional panel that's investigating synthetic drugs, so she needs to get up to speed on everything that's been happening during her absence. But thank you for your interest, and I'm sure we'll see you all soon."

More questions are shouted out, but Jason ushers me into the foyer and I must admit that I feel slightly relieved. I can handle the media, but I'm at my best when I'm hard at work.

"Oh, this came," Jason says quietly, handing me a card. "I thought you'd like to see it."

Looking down at the card, I see that it's an invitation from the company behind Hotel Necro:

We hope you enjoyed playing Escape From Hotel Necro. We have other unique experiences available at over 150 locations worldwide. Book before the end of the month and get 5% off.

"Interested?" Jason asks.

"I definitely could be," I reply, handing the card back to him. "Why don't you investigate and see if there's anything that looks good? If you find something, go ahead and book it. But not for any time before next May, because I'll just have too much on."

"Got it," he says, before giving me a kiss on the cheek. "Welcome back, by the way. To work, I mean. It's good to see you in your natural habitat, Elizabeth."

"It's good to *be* back in my natural habitat," I reply, before hesitating for a moment. "I know this might sound strange, but... Could you try calling me Lizzy?"

"Lizzy?" He seems a little startled. "You've never wanted to be called Lizzy. It's always been Elizabeth."

"I know," I say, "but I just thought maybe it'd be good to have a little change."

"Okay... Lizzy," he says, as if he's not quite convinced. "That's gonna take some getting used to. Now, if you'll excuse me, I have some research to -"

"There she is!" a voice shouts angrily. "There's the bitch who fired us!"

Turning, I see several people carrying boxes to the front door. These are obviously the I.T. people I decided to terminate last night, as part of our restructuring and streamlining process. We've offered them a good severance package and some long-term benefits, so I honestly don't understand how they can be so upset. I'm sure they'll all get other jobs very easily.

"You don't give a damn that we've got families to feed, do you?" one of the other men sneers as they all walk past. "How do you sleep at night?"

"Get them out of here!" Jason calls over to the security guards.

"No, wait," I say, stepping past him and looking at the I.T. man. "What did you just say to me?"

The man turns, and I can see the contempt in his eyes.

"You fire people with basically no warning," he says firmly. "You offer to extend our benefits, while taking them away from our families. You turf us out like we're rats. That's pretty cold. Hell, that's bordering on being a monster. I just don't get it. How do people like you sleep at night?"

I stare at him, and his words momentarily hurt before I take a deep breath and realize that this man is completely wrong. All the hurt quickly fades away.

"I sleep very well at night, actually," I say calmly, with a faint smile. "Thanks for asking."

Also by Amy Cross

The Devil, the Witch and the Whore
(The Deal book 1)

"Leave the forest alone. Whatever's out there, just let it be. Don't make it angry."

When a horrific discovery is made at the edge of town, Sheriff James Kopperud realizes the answers he seeks might be waiting beyond in the vast forest. But everybody in the town of Deal knows that there's something out there in the forest, something that should never be disturbed. A deal was made long ago, a deal that was supposed to keep the town safe. And if he insists on investigating the murder of a local girl, James is going to have to break that deal and head out into the wilderness.

Meanwhile, James has no idea that his estranged daughter Ramsey has returned to town. Ramsey is running from something, and she thinks she can find safety in the vast tunnel system that runs beneath the forest. Before long, however, Ramsey finds herself coming face to face with creatures that hide in the shadows. One of these creatures is known as the devil, and another is known as the witch. They're both waiting for the whore to arrive, but for very different reasons. And soon Ramsey is offered a terrible deal, one that could save or destroy the entire town, and maybe even the world.

Also by Amy Cross

The Soul Auction

"I saw a woman on the beach. I watched her face a demon."

Thirty years after her mother's death, Alice Ashcroft is drawn back to the coastal English town of Curridge. Somebody in Curridge has been reviewing Alice's novels online, and in those reviews there have been tantalizing hints at a hidden truth. A truth that seems to be linked to her dead mother.

"Thirty years ago, there was a soul auction."

Once she reaches Curridge, Alice finds strange things happening all around her. Something attacks her car. A figure watches her on the beach at night. And when she tries to find the person who has been reviewing her books, she makes a horrific discovery.

What really happened to Alice's mother thirty years ago? Who was she talking to, just moments before dropping dead on the beach? What caused a huge rockfall that nearly tore a nearby cliff-face in half? And what sinister presence is lurking in the grounds of the local church?

Also by Amy Cross

Darper Danver: The Complete First Series

Five years ago, three friends went to a remote cabin in the woods and tried to contact the spirit of a long-dead soldier. They thought they could control whatever happened next. They were wrong...

Newly released from prison, Cassie Briggs returns to Fort Powell, determined to get her life back on track. Soon, however, she begins to suspect that an ancient evil still lurks in the nearby cabin. Was the mysterious Darper Danver really destroyed all those years ago, or does her spirit still linger, waiting for a chance to return?

As Cassie and her ex-boyfriend Fisher are finally forced to face the truth about what happened in the cabin, they realize that Darper isn't ready to let go of their lives just yet. Meanwhile, a vengeful woman plots revenge for her brother's murder, and a New York ghost writer arrives in town to uncover the truth. Before long, strange carvings begin to appear around town and blood starts to flow once again.

Also by Amy Cross

The Ghost of Molly Holt

"Molly Holt is dead. There's nothing to fear in this house."

When three teenagers set out to explore an abandoned house in the middle of a forest, they think they've found the location where the infamous Molly Holt video was filmed.

They've found much more than that...

Tim doesn't believe in ghosts, but he has a crush on a girl who does. That's why he ends up taking her out to the house, and it's also why he lets her take his only flashlight. But as they explore the house together, Tim and Becky start to realize that something else might be lurking in the shadows.

Something that, ten years ago, suffered unimaginable pain.

Something that won't rest until a terrible wrong has been put right.

Also by Amy Cross

American Coven

He kidnapped three women and held them in his basement. He thought they couldn't fight back. He was wrong...

Snatched from the street near her home, Holly Carter is taken to a rural house and thrown down into a stone basement. She meets two other women who have also been kidnapped, and soon Holly learns about the horrific rituals that take place in the house. Eventually, she's called upstairs to take her place in the ice bath.

As her nightmare continues, however, Holly learns about a mysterious power that exists in the basement, and which the three women might be able to harness. When they finally manage to get through the metal door, however, the women have no idea that their fight for freedom is going to stretch out for more than a decade, or that it will culminate in a final, devastating demonstration of their new-found powers.

Also by Amy Cross

The Ash House

Why would anyone ever return to a haunted house?

For Diane Mercer the answer is simple. She's dying of cancer, and she wants to know once and for all whether ghosts are real.

Heading home with her young son, Diane is determined to find out whether the stories are real. After all, everyone else claimed to see and hear strange things in the house over the years. Everyone except Diane had some kind of experience in the house, or in the little ash house in the yard.

As Diane explores the house where she grew up, however, her son is exploring the yard and the forest. And while his mother might be struggling to come to terms with her own impending death, Daniel Mercer is puzzled by fleeting appearances of a strange little girl who seems drawn to the ash house, and by strange, rasping coughs that he keeps hearing at night.

The Ash House is a horror novel about a woman who desperately wants to know what will happen to her when she dies, and about a boy who uncovers the shocking truth about a young girl's murder.

Also by Amy Cross

Haunted

Twenty years ago, the ghost of a dead little girl drove Sheriff Michael Blaine to his death.

Now, that same ghost is coming for his daughter.

Returning to the small town where she grew up, Alex Roberts is determined to live a normal, quiet life. For the residents of Railham, however, she's an unwelcome reminder of the town's darkest hour.

Twenty years ago, nine-year-old Mo Garvey was found brutally murdered in a nearby forest. Everyone thinks that Alex's father was responsible, but if the killer was brought to justice, why is the ghost of Mo Garvey still after revenge?

And how far will the real killer go to protect his secret, when Alex starts getting closer to the truth?

Haunted is a horror novel about a woman who has to face her past, about a town that would rather forget, and about a little girl who refuses to let death stand in her way.

Also by Amy Cross

The Curse of Wetherley House

"If you walk through that door, Evil Mary will get you."

When she agrees to visit a supposedly haunted house with an old friend, Rosie assumes she'll encounter nothing more scary than a few creaks and bumps in the night. Even the legend of Evil Mary doesn't put her off. After all, she knows ghosts aren't real. But when Mary makes her first appearance, Rosie realizes she might already be trapped.

For more than a century, Wetherley House has been cursed. A horrific encounter on a remote road in the late 1800's has already caused a chain of misery and pain for all those who live at the house. Wetherley House was abandoned long ago, after a terrible discovery in the basement, something has remained undetected within its room. And even the local children know that Evil Mary waits in the house for anyone foolish enough to walk through the front door.

Before long, Rosie realizes that her entire life has been defined by the spirit of a woman who died in agony. Can she become the first person to escape Evil Mary, or will she fall victim to the same fate as the house's other occupants?

Also by Amy Cross

The Ghosts of Hexley Airport

Ten years ago, more than two hundred people died in a horrific plane crash at Hexley Airport.

Today, some say their ghosts still haunt the terminal building.

When she starts her new job at the airport, working a night shift as part of the security team, Casey assumes the stories about the place can't be true. Even when she has a strange encounter in a deserted part of the departure hall, she's certain that ghosts aren't real.

Soon, however, she's forced to face the truth. Not only is there something haunting the airport's buildings and tarmac, but a sinister force is working behind the scenes to replicate the circumstances of the original accident. And as a snowstorm moves in, Hexley Airport looks set to witness yet another disaster.

Also by Amy Cross

The Girl Who Never Came Back

Twenty years ago, Charlotte Abernathy vanished while playing near her family's house. Despite a frantic search, no trace of her was found until a year later, when the little girl turned up on the doorstep with no memory of where she'd been.

Today, Charlotte has put her mysterious ordeal behind her, even though she's never learned where she was during that missing year. However, when her eight-year-old niece vanishes in similar circumstances, a fully-grown Charlotte is forced to make a fresh attempt to uncover the truth.

Originally published in 2013, the fully revised and updated version of *The Girl Who Never Came Back* tells the harrowing story of a woman who thought she could forget her past, and of a little girl caught in the tangled web of a dark family secret.

Also by Amy Cross

Asylum
(The Asylum Trilogy book 1)

"No-one ever leaves Lakehurst. The staff, the patients, the ghosts... Once you're here, you're stuck forever."

After shooting her little brother dead, Annie Radford is sent to Lakehurst psychiatric hospital for assessment. Hearing voices in her head, Annie is forced to undergo experimental new treatments devised by a mysterious old man who lives in the hospital's attic. It soon becomes clear that the hospital's staff, led by the vicious Nurse Winter, are hiding something horrific at Lakehurst.

As Annie struggles to survive the hospital, she learns more about Nurse Winter's own story. Once a promising young medical student, Kirsten Winter also heard voices in her head. Voices that traveled a long way to reach her. Voices that have a plan of their own. Voices that will stop at nothing to get what they want.

What kind of signals are being transmitted from the basement of the hospital? Who is the old man in the attic? Why are living human brains kept in jars? And what is the dark secret that lurks at the heart of the hospital?

BOOKS BY AMY CROSS

1. Dark Season: The Complete First Series (2011)
2. Werewolves of Soho (Lupine Howl book 1) (2012)
3. Werewolves of the Other London (Lupine Howl book 2) (2012)
4. Ghosts: The Complete Series (2012)
5. Dark Season: The Complete Second Series (2012)
6. The Children of Black Annis (Lupine Howl book 3) (2012)
7. Destiny of the Last Wolf (Lupine Howl book 4) (2012)
8. Asylum (The Asylum Trilogy book 1) (2012)
9. Dark Season: The Complete Third Series (2013)
10. Devil's Briar (2013)
11. Broken Blue (The Broken Trilogy book 1) (2013)
12. The Night Girl (2013)
13. Days 1 to 4 (Mass Extinction Event book 1) (2013)
14. Days 5 to 8 (Mass Extinction Event book 2) (2013)
15. The Library (The Library Chronicles book 1) (2013)
16. American Coven (2013)
17. Werewolves of Sangreth (Lupine Howl book 5) (2013)
18. Broken White (The Broken Trilogy book 2) (2013)
19. Grave Girl (Grave Girl book 1) (2013)
20. Other People's Bodies (2013)
21. The Shades (2013)
22. The Vampire's Grave and Other Stories (2013)
23. Darper Danver: The Complete First Series (2013)
24. The Hollow Church (2013)
25. The Dead and the Dying (2013)
26. Days 9 to 16 (Mass Extinction Event book 3) (2013)
27. The Girl Who Never Came Back (2013)
28. Ward Z (The Ward Z Series book 1) (2013)
29. Journey to the Library (The Library Chronicles book 2) (2014)
30. The Vampires of Tor Cliff Asylum (2014)
31. The Family Man (2014)
32. The Devil's Blade (2014)
33. The Immortal Wolf (Lupine Howl book 6) (2014)
34. The Dying Streets (Detective Laura Foster book 1) (2014)
35. The Stars My Home (2014)
36. The Ghost in the Rain and Other Stories (2014)
37. Ghosts of the River Thames (The Robinson Chronicles book 1) (2014)
38. The Wolves of Cur'eath (2014)
39. Days 46 to 53 (Mass Extinction Event book 4) (2014)
40. The Man Who Saw the Face of the World (2014)

41. The Art of Dying (Detective Laura Foster book 2) (2014)
42. Raven Revivals (Grave Girl book 2) (2014)
43. Arrival on Thaxos (Dead Souls book 1) (2014)
44. Birthright (Dead Souls book 2) (2014)
45. A Man of Ghosts (Dead Souls book 3) (2014)
46. The Haunting of Hardstone Jail (2014)
47. A Very Respectable Woman (2015)
48. Better the Devil (2015)
49. The Haunting of Marshall Heights (2015)
50. Terror at Camp Everbee (The Ward Z Series book 2) (2015)
51. Guided by Evil (Dead Souls book 4) (2015)
52. Child of a Bloodied Hand (Dead Souls book 5) (2015)
53. Promises of the Dead (Dead Souls book 6) (2015)
54. Days 54 to 61 (Mass Extinction Event book 5) (2015)
55. Angels in the Machine (The Robinson Chronicles book 2) (2015)
56. The Curse of Ah-Qal's Tomb (2015)
57. Broken Red (The Broken Trilogy book 3) (2015)
58. The Farm (2015)
59. Fallen Heroes (Detective Laura Foster book 3) (2015)
60. The Haunting of Emily Stone (2015)
61. Cursed Across Time (Dead Souls book 7) (2015)
62. Destiny of the Dead (Dead Souls book 8) (2015)
63. The Death of Jennifer Kazakos (Dead Souls book 9) (2015)
64. Alice Isn't Well (Death Herself book 1) (2015)
65. Annie's Room (2015)
66. The House on Everley Street (Death Herself book 2) (2015)
67. Meds (The Asylum Trilogy book 2) (2015)
68. Take Me to Church (2015)
69. Ascension (Demon's Grail book 1) (2015)
70. The Priest Hole (Nykolas Freeman book 1) (2015)
71. Eli's Town (2015)
72. The Horror of Raven's Briar Orphanage (Dead Souls book 10) (2015)
73. The Witch of Thaxos (Dead Souls book 11) (2015)
74. The Rise of Ashalla (Dead Souls book 12) (2015)
75. Evolution (Demon's Grail book 2) (2015)
76. The Island (The Island book 1) (2015)
77. The Lighthouse (2015)
78. The Cabin (The Cabin Trilogy book 1) (2015)
79. At the Edge of the Forest (2015)
80. The Devil's Hand (2015)
81. The 13th Demon (Demon's Grail book 3) (2016)
82. After the Cabin (The Cabin Trilogy book 2) (2016)
83. The Border: The Complete Series (2016)
84. The Dead Ones (Death Herself book 3) (2016)

85. A House in London (2016)
86. Persona (The Island book 2) (2016)
87. Battlefield (Nykolas Freeman book 2) (2016)
88. Perfect Little Monsters and Other Stories (2016)
89. The Ghost of Shapley Hall (2016)
90. The Blood House (2016)
91. The Death of Addie Gray (2016)
92. The Girl With Crooked Fangs (2016)
93. Last Wrong Turn (2016)
94. The Body at Auercliff (2016)
95. The Printer From Hell (2016)
96. The Dog (2016)
97. The Nurse (2016)
98. The Haunting of Blackwych Grange (2016)
99. Twisted Little Things and Other Stories (2016)
100. The Horror of Devil's Root Lake (2016)
101. The Disappearance of Katie Wren (2016)
102. B&B (2016)
103. The Bride of Ashbyrn House (2016)
104. The Devil, the Witch and the Whore (The Deal Trilogy book 1) (2016)
105. The Ghosts of Lakeforth Hotel (2016)
106. The Ghost of Longthorn Manor and Other Stories (2016)
107. Laura (2017)
108. The Murder at Skellin Cottage (Jo Mason book 1) (2017)
109. The Curse of Wetherley House (2017)
110. The Ghosts of Hexley Airport (2017)
111. The Return of Rachel Stone (Jo Mason book 2) (2017)
112. Haunted (2017)
113. The Vampire of Downing Street and Other Stories (2017)
114. The Ash House (2017)
115. The Ghost of Molly Holt (2017)
116. The Camera Man (2017)
117. The Soul Auction (2017)
118. The Abyss (The Island book 3) (2017)
119. Broken Window (The House of Jack the Ripper book 1) (2017)
120. In Darkness Dwell (The House of Jack the Ripper book 2) (2017)
121. Cradle to Grave (The House of Jack the Ripper book 3) (2017)
122. The Lady Screams (The House of Jack the Ripper book 4) (2017)
123. A Beast Well Tamed (The House of Jack the Ripper book 5) (2017)
124. Doctor Charles Grazier (The House of Jack the Ripper book 6) (2017)
125. The Raven Watcher (The House of Jack the Ripper book 7) (2017)
126. The Final Act (The House of Jack the Ripper book 8) (2017)
127. Stephen (2017)
128. The Spider (2017)

129. The Mermaid's Revenge (2017)
130. The Girl Who Threw Rocks at the Devil (2018)
131. Friend From the Internet (2018)
132. Beautiful Familiar (2018)
133. One Night at a Soul Auction (2018)
134. 16 Frames of the Devil's Face (2018)
135. The Haunting of Caldgrave House (2018)
136. Like Stones on a Crow's Back (The Deal Trilogy book 2) (2018)
137. Room 9 and Other Stories (2018)
138. The Gravest Girl of All (Grave Girl book 3) (2018)
139. Return to Thaxos (Dead Souls book 13) (2018)
140. The Madness of Annie Radford (The Asylum Trilogy book 3) (2018)
141. The Haunting of Briarwych Church (Briarwych book 1) (2018)
142. I Just Want You To Be Happy (2018)
143. Day 100 (Mass Extinction Event book 6) (2018)
144. The Horror of Briarwych Church (Briarwych book 2) (2018)
145. The Ghost of Briarwych Church (Briarwych book 3) (2018)
146. Lights Out (2019)
147. Apocalypse (The Ward Z Series book 3) (2019)
148. Days 101 to 108 (Mass Extinction Event book 7) (2019)
149. The Haunting of Daniel Bayliss (2019)
150. The Purchase (2019)
151. Harper's Hotel Ghost Girl (Death Herself book 4) (2019)
152. The Haunting of Aldburn House (2019)
153. Days 109 to 116 (Mass Extinction Event book 8) (2019)
154. Bad News (2019)
155. The Wedding of Rachel Blaine (2019)
156. Dark Little Wonders and Other Stories (2019)
157. The Music Man (2019)
158. The Vampire Falls (Three Nights of the Vampire book 1) (2019)
159. The Other Ann (2019)
160. The Butcher's Husband and Other Stories (2019)
161. The Haunting of Lannister Hall (2019)
162. The Vampire Burns (Three Nights of the Vampire book 2) (2019)
163. Days 195 to 202 (Mass Extinction Event book 9) (2019)

For more information, visit:

www. amycross.com

Printed in Great Britain
by Amazon